THE TIME STANDS STILL CHRONICLES

Book # 2

Masters of Time

By D.A. Lee

The Time Stands Still Chronicles: Masters of Time
By D.A. Lee

Published by Time Stands Still Press, LLC
www.TimeStandsStillChronicles.com

Time Stands Still Press books are available from Ingram Press
and can be ordered through Ingram Press.

This book is a work of fiction. Names, characters, places, and incidents either are products of the author's imagination or are used fictitiously. Any resemblance to actual events or locales or persons, living or dead, is merely coincidental.

LLCN: 2013930216

ISBN: 978-0-9846957-2-0

Dedication

For Ben and Erin, my two wonderful kids who have enriched my life immeasurably. You have been and continue to be a joy and blessing in my life.

Acknowledgments

Thanks again to Susan, my wife, for your tireless reading and listening to the manuscript. Your copy edit ideas were insightful and useful. I couldn't have done it without you.

1

"I must return to Saros tonight," Dr. M stated. "There have been some significant developments. There is more talk and plans are being made for an invasion. The water shortage is getting more serious. While I am there, I will pick up two more Saros stones. One will be for Mike. Have you determined who the fourth member of the team will be?"

"Erika," they both said at the same time.

"Good. Then we are done for now. I will contact you when I return to Earth."

Two weeks later...

The last day of school had finally arrived at Millville Elementary School. Dr. Green had announced last week that the fourth, fifth, and sixth graders would have a picnic in the afternoon on the last day of school. It would last from 12:30 until 2:30 out on the fields. He also reminded everyone of the class races that would take place at two o'clock.

The weather cooperated and the temperature was topping out at a perfect 72 degrees. It was a beautiful day to be outside. All the teachers had organized things for their classes to do. Some played softball, some kickball, and some soccer. One class had set up on the basketball court and was having shooting contests. Everyone was having a great time.

At 1:50, Dr. Green used his bullhorn and called everyone over to the field where the races were to be run. Each class had selected their fastest boy and girl for a race two times around the cones that the physical education teacher had set up. He had no idea disaster was about to strike!

. . . .

All the students were shouting and screaming at the runners. The girls' race was being run, and all the fifth graders yelled Sandie's name as she crossed the finish line first.

"Yeah, Sandie!" the kids all yelled. "You sure showed those sixth graders! Way to go!"

All twenty-five kids from Sandie's class rushed to her just past the finish line. Each student wanted to hug and congratulate her. The excitement was contagious.

Finally, Dr. Green had to use his bullhorn to get the kids off the track so the next race could be run. He began calling for the boys to line up.

Then the race started.

"Run, Billy, run!" someone shouted.

"Go, Mike!" someone else yelled.

The race was about half over as the faster runners passed the finish line for the first time. Only one lap left for them.

Four or five runners were just rounding the last curve, still on their first lap. Suddenly, one of the boys was quickly being left behind. As he approached the finish line, his face was beet red, and he was really puffing. He seemed to be unable to get a breath. He collapsed as he crossed the line and did not move.

"He's dead! I think he's dead!" Pat, a fifth grade student, yelled out. He was leaning out over the collapsed fourth grader on the track. All three hundred fifty kids were completely hushed after seeing Sammy fall down on the track during the race and not get up. It happened right in front of the finish line, so most of the kids saw it.

Dr. Green had quickly rushed over to the fallen student. He lowered his head to check his breathing. Sammy wasn't breathing.

"Here, let me help," ordered Mrs. Matthews who was the school nurse. "I'll start CPR. Dr. Green, you call 9-1-1."

"Okay," he replied, still shaken by what had happened. After calling 9-1-1 on his cell phone, he announced, "Teachers, please take your students back into your classrooms."

Slowly and very quietly, the shocked students walked back into the building. There was only a half hour left of the school year, and something awful had happened.

The paramedics arrived in seven minutes. They worked on Sammy for several minutes.

"It looks like his heart just stopped beating," one of the paramedics finally said. "There's nothing we can do for him now. He's dead."

They loaded him onto the stretcher and took him to the ambulance. Then they drove to the hospital.

Sammy's mom had been called right after the paramedics. She arrived after the ambulance had pulled away. It was hard for Mrs. Matthews to tell her that her son was dead.

She burst into tears. "Oh, no! Not my baby!" sobbed Sammy's mother. "There must be some mistake!" Mrs. Matthews put an arm around her and led her to the parking lot.

"Nurse Matthews, will you please call my husband at work? I don't think I could keep from crying if I called him. Here's a card with his number on it."

"Sure. I'll explain what happened, and he can meet you at the hospital."

"Thank you," Sammy's mom replied as she continued to wipe away the tears.

Meanwhile, the students were somewhat in shock in their classrooms. They had heard the student say he thought Sammy was dead before Dr. Green could get to him. Everyone was sad, and many students in Sammy's classroom were crying.

The same calmness that Henri had felt in the convenience store had just come over J.J. His sixth-grade class was a little noisy as Dr. M had allowed the students to talk and get their feelings out. He was puzzled at the way he felt, sort of distracted, apart from everyone in the room. His seat was in the back so no one could really see him well.

I hope this works, he thought to himself. He pressed his right thumb into the stone on his bracelet. There it was again. Something flashed, and he sort of blinked…just like before with Mike.

J.J. did not know how long it had been since the accident and wondered if too much time had passed for him to go back and try to change what happened. Luckily, only a half hour or so had passed.

The girls were bunched up at the starting line and the race began again. The students were shouting and screaming at the runners. All the fifth graders yelled Sandie's name as she crossed the finish line first.

"Yeah, Sandie!" the kids all yelled. "You sure showed those sixth graders! Way to go!"

All twenty-five kids from Sandie's class rushed to her just past the finish line. Each student wanted to hug and congratulate her. The excitement was contagious.

Finally, Dr. Green had to use his bullhorn to get the kids off the track so the next race could be run.

Things were going to happen fast now. Dr. Green was already calling for the boys to line up. And there was Sammy at the starting line. J.J. had to think fast.

He didn't know how he could stop the race. He could yell, "Snake!" And that would disrupt things. But that would just get him in trouble, and the race would still be run with the same disastrous result.

Suddenly, an idea came to him. He ran as fast as he could to the building and through the outside halls to the office. Luckily, the nurse's office was the first room just inside the main doors. Otherwise, someone would have stopped him for running inside the building.

There it was, right on the wall, the defibrillator, all packaged up in a case, ready to be taken where needed. He grabbed it and ran back out to the athletic field where nearly everyone was watching the race.

"Run, Billy, run!" someone shouted.

"Go, Mike!" someone else yelled.

The race was about half over as the faster runners passed the finish line for the first time. Only one lap left for them.

Four or five runners were just rounding the last curve, still on their first lap. Sammy was among them but was quickly being left behind. He obviously was in distress. As he approached the finish line, his face was beet red, and he was really puffing. He seemed to be unable to get a breath.

"Mrs. Matthews!" screamed J.J. "Sammy's in trouble at the finish line! It looks like he can't breathe!"

As Mrs. Matthews turned from the teacher she was talking to and looked at the runners, she saw Sammy collapse. J.J. was nearly to him when Sammy hit the ground and lay still. He quickly opened the defibrillator case and took out the unit.

Dr. Green had rushed over to the fallen student. He lowered his head to check his breathing. Sammy wasn't breathing.

Mrs. Matthews was there in an instant. "Here, I'll do that," she exclaimed as she took the unit and spread it out next to Sammy. She turned the unit on. "Dr. Green, call 9-1-1." Then she examined Sammy. She saw that he wasn't breathing. She could feel no pulse. So she did the only thing she could do. "Stay back. Don't touch anything." She put the pads on Sammy's upper left chest and lower right. She checked the gauge that showed the unit was charged and ready. "Clear," she said and hit the button, sending a charge of electricity through Sammy's chest. Still no heartbeat.

She checked the indicator gauge. It showed that the unit had recharged. "I'm trying it again. Clear!" she warned. Another charge and again Sammy's body bounced off the ground. But this time Sammy's mouth came open. She leaned over and put her head next to his chest. His heart was beating.

"Teachers, please take your students back into the building and into your classrooms," Dr. Green announced using his bullhorn.

Slowly and very quietly, the shocked students walked back into the building. There was only a half hour left in the school year, and something awful had happened.

Nurse Matthews checked Sammy's breathing, and it was very shallow, barely noticeable. She quickly removed the defibrillator pads and started CPR. She kept that up until someone said, "We'll take over now, ma'am." The new voice told her that the paramedics had arrived. She was exhausted.

Mrs. Matthews let out a sigh of relief. "His heart stopped beating after running a race. I used the defibrillator twice, and that got his heart beating again. His breathing was very shallow, so I started CPR."

After several minutes, the uniformed paramedic said, "You did everything right. You saved this boy's life!"

One of the other paramedics had already started an IV in Sammy's wrist. He was also hooked up to another machine that one of the paramedics was taking readings from. She was relaying the information back to a doctor at the hospital.

Two other paramedics returned from their emergency vehicle with a stretcher. Once they got the okay from the lead paramedic, they carefully hoisted Sammy onto the stretcher.

"What happened, Mrs. Matthews?" Sammy suddenly said. "Where am I?"

"You're just fine, Sammy. You're on the school playground. You had a little fall. These nice paramedics are going to take good care of you. Oh, look! Here comes your mom."

Sammy's mom had been called right after the 9-1-1 call had been made.

"Mrs. Matthews, what happened? Why is Sammy hooked up to those machines?" she asked worriedly.

"Easy, Mrs. Cole. Sammy fell and was unconscious. They're taking him to the hospital for further examination. They think he will be all right."

"Are you the boy's mother?" the lead paramedic asked.

"Yes, sir, I am," she replied, still shocked.

"The nurse is right, ma'am. The doctor at the hospital just wants to take a look at Sammy to be sure everything is okay. His vital signs all look good. You can ride along with your son if you want to."

"Yes, I certainly want to do that!" she exclaimed as she wiped the tears from her eyes. "Nurse Matthews, will you please call my husband at work? I don't think I could keep from crying if I called him. Here's a card with his number on it."

"Sure. I'll explain what happened, and he can meet you at the hospital. They'll tell you more after the doctor examines Sammy. Just try to relax. Sammy is going to be all right."

"Hey, Mom. Are we going to ride in an ambulance?" Sammy asked. "That'll be fun!" He sounded like his old self again.

"Yes, we are, son. They want the doctor to check you over just to be sure there's nothing wrong."

"I feel fine. Although I do feel very tired."

Sammy was asleep by the time they got him to the ambulance.

"He's doing fine," one of the paramedics commented as they climbed into the rescue vehicle. "Sleeping will be good for him."

Nurse Matthews was able to get the paramedic's information to Dr. Green before school was dismissed for the summer. He made the happy announcement three minutes before dismissal.

"I'm very happy to tell you that Sammy is awake and talking with his mom and the paramedics. They tell me they think Sammy will be okay. We're sorry we had to interrupt our race, but I'm sure we are all glad Sammy is okay. An information sheet is being delivered to your teachers for you to take home to your parents. It will explain what happened to Sammy. Be sure you give it to your parents and talk with them about it.

"Everyone have a safe and enjoyable summer. You sixth graders will be missed. I wish you success in middle school. I'll see all the rest of you right back here when school starts after Labor Day!"

With that J.J. got up and left the classroom, heading for the doors and preparing to leave elementary school for the last time.

Cheers could be heard all over the school. The good news about Sammy was a welcome way to end the school year. Happy kids could be seen leaving the school from nearly every door in the building. Summer vacation was finally here.

As J.J. and Mike were walking toward the exit doors, Nurse Matthews called out, "J.J. and Mike, can I see you boys for a minute? It won't take long."

The boys walked into the nurse's office. She had no way of knowing that J.J. had been in there earlier on a desperate mercy mission.

"Mike, could you wait out here in my outer office? I want to talk with J.J. He was the first one to get to Sammy after he collapsed."

"Sure, Nurse Matthews, I'll wait here."

Uh-oh, thought J.J., *here it comes. She's going to want to know why I had the defibrillator outside.*

"That was good thinking, J.J., to have brought the defibrillator outside. I should have thought of that. I always like to be prepared. You saved Sammy's life today."

"Oh, I think you did that. I wasn't even sure how to use that machine," he lied. "I just hoped you weren't upset with me for taking it outside. I thought we might need it. I don't want to be treated like a hero. We worked together to help Sammy."

"You're some young man, J.J. I wish we had more students like you at this school. We're going to miss you."

"Just keep looking around, Nurse Matthews. There are great people all around you."

"You have a good summer, J.J. Come back and see us some time."

"Goodbye, Nurse Matthews. You have a good summer, too."

2

AT ABOUT 6:00 P.M. ON THE DAY SCHOOL LET OUT FOR summer, J.J. was sitting on his back porch. He needed some time alone. He had just saved another life thanks to his use of the special stone. And he couldn't tell anyone about it. That made it even harder to understand. He knew there would be unscrupulous people who would want to use his power for greed. Someone could make a lot of money if they knew the outcome of a race or professional contest beforehand. He wondered if the power would work for such things. He hoped it wouldn't.

What am I going to do? he thought. *I wish there were some way I could talk about this with someone.*

Just then the telephone rang. J.J. went in to answer it. It was Grams.

"Hi, J.J. Did you have a big day at school today?"

"What do you mean, Grams?" J.J. replied as an enigmatic expression appeared on his face. "It was just the last day before summer vacation."

"Why don't we talk about this tomorrow? It's Friday and your mom can drop you off for a short visit. We can have a nice talk. Your mom said you have something to show me as well as something to ask me."

J.J. was aghast. Grams sounded like she knew a lot more than she was telling. He hesitatingly agreed. "Okay. I'll ask Mom when she gets home. What time should I come?"

"How about eleven o'clock? I'll have some sandwiches, and we can have lunch out on the front porch. Tell your mom you'll be here about an hour. Don't worry. There's nothing wrong. Actually, everything is turning out very well. See you tomorrow." And she hung up.

Now, I'm scared, J.J. thought. *I'll have to show her the bracelet and apologize. I wonder if she'll let me keep it. What will I do if she tells me I have to give it back to her? What about the special power it has? Should I tell her about it? Oh, dear. I'm confused.* His tenuous hold over his emotions gave way, and a tear slipped out of his eye and ran down his cheek.

"Hi, son," called his mom from the kitchen. She had just come home from work. "Oh, my! Is that a tear?"

"Mom, I'm worried about talking with Grams. She just called and wants me to come out and talk tomorrow. I'm afraid she knows about the bracelet. Did you tell her? Is she mad at me?"

"No, son. I didn't tell her about the bracelet. You must trust Grams. She's a very wise lady. I'm sure she won't be mad at you. I can take you out tomorrow morning. I don't have to work. What time does she want you there?"

"She said to come out at eleven o'clock, and she would have sandwiches ready for lunch. She'd like to have me stay for about an hour or so."

"That will work just fine for me. Don't give this another thought. I'm sure Grams will put you right at ease. She's wonderful."

. . . .

Henri, her mom, and Joey had a nice supper together. Harriet, her mother, was a great cook.

"Mom, that beef roast was wonderful. I think I ate enough for two people. And those sweet potatoes! What did you put in them? They were incredibly sweet."

"I cooked the potatoes with brown sugar and some syrup," she replied smiling. She liked it when the kids appreciated her cooking.

"Dessert was the best part. That apple pie was scrumptious." Joey grinned after using such a big word. "The ice cream made it even cooler," he added, still grinning.

"Very clever, young man," his mom complimented. "What's on the agenda this evening for you two?"

It was Thursday evening, but there was no school tomorrow. Summer vacation was starting.

"I think I'll stay up until midnight. I don't want to miss the first minutes of my summer vacation," Joey suggested.

"Oh, no, you won't. We'll adjust your bedtime to ten o'clock for the summer. Fridays you can stay up until 10:30. That's the limit," Mom said firmly.

"I guess ten o'clock is better than nine o'clock," came Joey's reply. "Although I am a third grader now," he added proudly.

"You still need lots of sleep. You'll probably grow an inch or two this summer. You don't want to be too tired to enjoy being taller, do you?" Mom jokingly replied.

"Guess I'll just go play video games until ten o'clock then."

Henri jumped into the conversation. "It's only 7:30, but I'm really tired. I think I'll read and see if I fall asleep."

"Good night then. I'll come up just before ten o'clock to see how you both are doing," Mom added.

"Good night, Mom," Henri said. Joey was already up the stairs and in his room. He enjoyed his video games and couldn't wait to play them.

Henri decided she would take a shower before reading. Then she thought, *A nice hot bubble bath would be even better.* So she took off her pullover blouse and tossed it onto her bed. She sat down at her vanity to brush her hair first. While brushing, she was startled when she noticed that the necklace around her neck was missing.

She looked down and was relieved to see the necklace right there, hanging on the strap around her neck. "What's this?" she softly asked herself. She looked up and stared into the mirror again. The necklace was not there. "How is this possible?"

Next, she got a small handheld mirror from her left dresser drawer. She looked down and saw the necklace. She looked at the reflection in the mirror she was holding and saw nothing. The necklace had no reflection.

"I wonder if this means no one else can see my necklace?" she said very quietly. "That seems impossible. It would save me answering questions about it, though. I'll have to either find a way to check it out or just ask Gramma Tessie."

She put on a white sleeveless blouse and put the necklace on the outside. Then she went downstairs to get a drink. She hoped to run into her mom and see if she noticed the necklace. Good fortune was with her as her mom was pulling the dishes out of the dishwasher and putting them away.

"Hi, Henri. Need something?" she said looking up. "That's a pretty blouse."

"Just needed a drink. I was about to take a bath and just pulled it on to wear downstairs. I was thinking about wearing it to church on Sunday. Do you think I need to wear a necklace with it?"

"I think a necklace would look great with it. But it looks okay without one, too."

"Thanks, Mom. Can I help with the dishes?"

"No, I'm almost finished."

Henri got her drink and turned to face her mom. "Thanks again for a great supper. See you in the morning."

Mom looked right at Henri again and replied, "Sleep tight," and went back to putting the dishes away.

She didn't see the necklace, Henri thought as she went upstairs.

Once upstairs, she knocked on Joey's door. She knocked again, louder. Finally, he came to the door. "What do you want?" he asked angrily.

"I just wanted to know what you think of the color of this blouse. Do you think I should I wear a necklace with it?"

"The color sucks! And yes, you should get a necklace to go with it. That might help a lot. It looks dumb without one." With that he closed his door.

Joey was usually a nice, friendly little brother. However, he did not like to be interrupted while playing his video games.

Back in her room, Henri was mystified. *Why didn't Gramma Tessie tell me about the necklace?* she thought. *No one can see it but me. But then how did Gramma see it?* Henri had no answers.

Maybe that hot bath is just what I need, she thought. So down the hall and into the bathroom she went. She locked the door. Joey could go downstairs if he needed a bathroom.

She was right. The hot bath really relaxed her. She dried off, put on her robe, and returned to her room. Now, she was ready to sleep. Everything would work out. She just knew it.

3

It was the evening before J.J., Mom, and Jerry were going to Gram's house. J.J. was upstairs in his room getting ready for bed. He went into the bathroom to brush his teeth. When he had finished, he used his hands to brush his hair back.

That's strange, he thought. He couldn't see the bracelet in the mirror. *I'm sure I didn't take it off,* he thought. He brought his hands up in front of his face, and the bracelet was right there on his wrist. When he looked back into the mirror, it was gone again. *Why is there no reflection in the mirror?* he thought to himself.

He thought of a way to test this reflection thing out. He walked over to his brother's room and knocked on the door. J.J. had drawn a plus sign and a times sign inside a circle on his left arm using a water-based marker. Then he had pulled the bracelet over the drawing.

When Jerry opened the door, J.J. held out his arm. "Jer, what do you think of my new tattoo?"

"It looks kind of silly. Isn't it just a plus sign and a times sign inside a circle?"

"Yes, that's all it is. I think I'll wash it off."

J.J. was astonished. When he returned to his room, he whispered out loud, "He couldn't see the bracelet. It's become invisible to everyone but me." He tried the mirror test again and the bracelet was invisible in the mirror. This was a strange occurrence.

He decided there was nothing he could do about it. At least he would not have to answer questions about the old bracelet he was wearing.

"But how can I show it to Grams if she can't see it? Oh, boy. What a mess this is," he whispered to himself again. "Well, I'll start with the old Bible from the basement. I'll see how that goes. Maybe I'll think of something before tomorrow morning."

Thinking it would be hard to sleep, he turned on some music. Within minutes, he was sound asleep. The bracelet on his wrist glowed for a few seconds and then went dark again.

They were all up early on Friday. No one knew why. It was only eight o'clock when they all met in the kitchen. Mom had asked Jerry to ride along to drop J.J. off. Then they would drive another ten miles over to Davisburg to a big farmers' market. Jerry could help her pick out the fruits and vegetables she wanted. It would take just enough time for Grams and J.J. to talk.

Mom cooked scrambled eggs, ham, potatoes, and cheese together in her big frying pan. She asked Jerry to make toast while J.J. poured the orange juice.

"Grams expects us at eleven o'clock this morning, so let's plan to leave around 10:45," Mom said. "Jerry and I are going fruit and vegetable shopping at Davisburg. We'll be back to get you between 12:15 and 12:30. Grams told me that would be just fine with her."

"Okay, Mom," J.J. replied. "Grams said she would have some cookies out for us to snack on as well as lunch. We'll try to save some cookies for you and Jerry," he said with a crooked smile.

"Knowing Grams, she'll have plenty of cookies for everyone."

They finished breakfast, and the boys put the dishes into the dishwasher. Mom said she'd take care of the frying pan. She wanted to let it cool before washing it.

The boys came down the stairs at 10:35. "Anything we can do?" they asked.

"No," Mom replied. "I'll be ready in a few minutes. You two go outside and wait for me."

"Okay," they replied together.

They arrived at Gram's farm a minute or two early. She waved to them from the front porch. Mom honked the horn, and Jerry waved from the backseat as J.J. got out. He said goodbye to Mom and Jerry and headed for the porch. Mom drove around the circle driveway and took off for the farmers' market.

"Hi, J.J.," Grams said with a warm smile. "I'm so glad you could come out so soon. Come inside and help me carry the sandwiches and cookies out here."

Soon they were seated on the porch, just the two of them way out here in the country. No one could hear what they would say. Grams had already made sure of that.

"Let me try to put you at ease right away. I'm sure you are going to be surprised at this. I know that you have just saved Mike and Sammy's lives. I also know that you are wearing a very powerful invisible bracelet. In fact, I know you are wearing it right now." She paused to let J.J. digest this information. "You are a unique young man, and you will do a lot more special and important things in the future."

"How do you know this? Can you see the bracelet?" He was incredulous. *She's just my grandmother, isn't she?* he thought.

"I can't tell you very much right now. There are two other people who know about your power. You will be talking with each of them in the near future. They will contact you. Don't be afraid. We're all on the same team. We'll all be working together soon. We have a leader who will be the last to contact you, probably when summer is over or sometime during the next year. If events push our timetable up, he will contact you sooner. There will be no doubt in your mind who your team members are when they are ready to talk with you."

"I don't understand this team stuff. I don't understand any of this." He was overwhelmed.

"Did you like the feeling when you saved your friend, Mike?"

"Well, I don't know what I felt. I sure was glad he didn't die. So, yes, I guess it felt good."

"How did you feel about saving Sammy, someone you didn't even know?"

"I guess that felt good, too."

"Do you want to continue doing good deeds and maybe even save many more lives?"

"I guess so. Is that what I'm going to do?"

"Is that something you want to do?"

"Sure. It just seems so impossible!"

"You don't need to think about it right now. Just let things happen. It's like that bracelet. It's become a part of you. You can see it and touch it, but no one else can. They will not even feel it if they touch your arm right where it's at. That's to protect you from people who would want to use your power for evil purposes."

"This sounds like something I'd read about in a science fiction book. Will I wake up tomorrow and discover this was all a dream?"

"You will wake up tomorrow just like every other day. Live each day just as you have been. Things will work out for you. Don't try to plan any uses of your power. It will be there to work for you when you need it. The hardest part will be not telling anyone about what you have done."

"Can I talk with you about it?"

"Only when I bring it up first. We don't want anyone overhearing our conversations."

"Who would hear us out here on the farm?"

"There is evil everywhere. We can't take any chances. You will know much more and have a little better understanding about all of this by the end of summer vacation. You will also have someone else you can share things with very soon. That should make it much easier for you. Someone else will want to share with you about his or her power. You will work together."

"That sounds a little better. I'd sure like to be able to share this with someone."

"Try to be patient. That will happen soon enough. Oh, look. Your Mom and Jerry are coming."

"Wow! Where did the time go? I haven't even eaten one cookie. I think I'll have one now."

"Tell your mom we talked about a lot of things. Tell her I needed to have the bracelet back. She'll understand. However, she knows nothing about it or its power. She is not to know anything about our little talk, okay?"

"Sure, Grams. I don't think she'd believe me anyway."

"That's good. I think I'll have a cookie now, too."

"Mom. Look at all the cookies! Can I have some?" Jerry asked as he climbed onto the porch and picked up two cookies.

"You sure may," replied Grams with a smile. "Here's a bag. Why don't you put a dozen inside and take them with you. I have another bag here for J.J., too."

"Gee, thanks, Grams!" exclaimed Jerry as he came over and kissed Grams on the cheek.

"Don't I get any?" Mrs. Jamison asked.

"You, my dear daughter, get the large bag of cookies sitting on the counter in the kitchen. There are a couple of dozen cookies there for you. Enjoy!"

"Thanks, Mom," she replied. "I think I'll use the restroom and then we'll be going."

Soon the three of them were in the car heading back to Millville. J.J. rubbed his eyes and already wondered if his talk with Grams had been a dream. He fell asleep on the way home even though it was only a three-mile drive.

4

Erika and Henri were finally going to have that swimming party Gramma Tessie had promised. Besides her younger brother, Joey, Tessie had invited Mike and J.J., J.J.'s younger brother, Jerry, and Mike's older brother, Daryl. Daryl was told he could invite his good friend, Hank, who worked at Deano's.

Mr. and Mrs. Sorenson were also coming to the party. They had both worked as lifeguards and were excellent swimmers. They would sit on the shore most of the time and watch the kids have all the fun. Mr. Sorenson would swim out to the raft occasionally to cool off.

By two o'clock on Saturday one week after school was out, everyone was on the beach at Tessie's place. The two picnic tables were covered with coolers and towels.

"Let's get wet!" shouted Mike.

"I'll be the first one in," replied Erika. She quickly pulled off her shorts and blouse to reveal a dark green one-piece swimsuit. She ran to the end of the dock and carefully dove in. She had swum here before and knew how to dive in safely.

Mike and J.J. were just a few steps behind her. Splash! Splash! Both Mike and J.J. had done cannonballs. They both also had hit bottom.

"Ouch!" yelled Mike. He was heavier than J.J. "That hurt."

"Well, chubby, that's what you get from eating all the time. You sink faster," kidded J.J.

The two boys recovered and swam out to the raft where Erika sat waiting. "What took you so long?" she asked.

Mike and J.J. grinned sheepishly. "We took a detour to the bottom of the lake on our way out here." They both laughed.

Jerry and Joey were content to jump in feet first from the dock. The water there only came up to their waists. There was also a small sandy beach where they could play with pails and shovels.

Daryl and Hank took their time getting ready to swim. Finally, they slipped into the water from the dock and walked partway out to the raft. They were too tall to dive in from the dock.

Gramma Tessie sat in a comfortable chair under a tree right near the edge of the lake. Erika's parents, Jim and Pat Sorenson, were sitting with her. They were getting ready to swim.

"I bought a new swimsuit just for this party," Pat announced. "I hope it's not too bright." She literally glowed as the sun gleamed off her bright yellow one-piece suit.

"You look great!" admired her husband. He had on his old solid dark blue swim trunks. At least their colors didn't clash. They waded into the water together and swam toward the raft.

Gramma Tessie got up and walked over to a small covered table. She pulled off the tarp to reveal three bright red inner tubes and two long blue rafts. She rolled the inner tubes down the slight incline and into the water. She carried the rafts and set them into the water, too.

"Those look like fun," Mike shouted as he dove off the raft and swam toward shore. Henri and Erika did the same. Soon all three were swimming back toward the raft with their toys.

Jerry and Joey grabbed the rafts and were playing with them as Tessie spoke, "You two have fun with those. Just don't go out past the raft with them. The water is over your heads out there," she cautioned.

"Oh, we won't," said Joey. "I don't like deep water. It's scary."

"We'll just float around here by the shore," added Jerry. "We want to make some sand castles in a few minutes."

"Have fun," replied Gramma Tessie.

"Let's play 'King of the Raft,'" Mike announced.

Pat and Jim both spoke at the same time. "First, give us your inner tubes and no roughhousing."

"Anyone who doesn't want to play needs to get into the water," Mike warned. Henri, J.J., Mike, Daryl, and Hank stayed on the raft. Now, it was a contest to see who could throw whom into the water.

Mike and J.J. both went after Henri. They succeeded in pushing her off the raft, but she grabbed J.J.'s arm and pulled him in along with her. Now, Mike was left on the raft with the two older boys. He didn't stand a chance. Daryl grabbed him by the arm and pulled him toward the edge of the raft. Then Hank said, "Let me help." But instead of trying to help, he pushed both Mike and Daryl into the lake.

Daryl came up choking after swallowing some lake water and getting it up his nose. "Nice goin'," he gargled as Mike pushed and Hank pulled to get him safely onto the raft. After several more coughs, he was finally okay.

"No more 'King of the Raft,'" ordered Jim. "Let's just swim and float and have a good time."

"We'd just like to sit on the raft and sun bathe," Erika said. Henri agreed.

The boys had fun jumping and diving off the raft. They tried to do cannonballs right near the edge of the raft to splash the girls. They were somewhat successful. The girls didn't seem to mind.

Finally, after a short time, the boys swam to shore, leaving the girls alone on the raft. They just bathed in the sun for the next forty-five minutes.

Jerry and Joey had created some really cool sand castles. They got the sand wet and used the pails to make mounds. Then they shaped the wet sand.

Pat and Jim sat down and talked with Tessie in the shade of a giant umbrella. They drank the lemonade Tessie had made.

Daryl and Hank just sat at the end of the dock, talking while dangling their legs in the water. It was a perfect day at the lake.

Without the other knowing, Henri and J.J. were having the same thoughts. They wondered if some disaster would happen while they were at the lake. Then J.J. remembered Grams admonishing him not to try to look for ways to use his power. Henri decided not to think about it anymore. So they just enjoyed their time at the lake.

Tessie, Pat, and Jim got the grill going. Erika and Henri safely swam in from the raft. Soon everyone was enjoying burgers and dogs with all the trimmings.

When the kids were full, everyone sat down to talk and rest. It was getting on towards five o'clock. Soon it would be time to go home.

No emergencies came up. No lives to save. Just a bunch of kids who had come to the lake, had fun, and were going home safely.

"This has been a fabulous day, Henri. Thanks for inviting me!" Erika commented on the way home. Henri was riding home with Erika and her parents while Mike, J.J., Jerry, and Joey were riding home with J.J.'s mom.

"You're welcome," Henri replied. "Let's try to do this once a week all summer. We can ride our bikes out and spend most of the day on the beach, in the water, and on the raft. Think of the tans we'll get."

"What do you think, Mom and Dad?"

"As long as Gramma Tessie doesn't mind, we won't," replied Mr. Sorenson. "Right, Honey?"

At that moment, a very strange feeling came over Henri. She didn't know what it was, except that it caused her to turn away from Erika and reach inside her sweatshirt and pull out her necklace. She held it in both hands, preparing to use it to stop time.

Why am I doing this? she thought. *I see no reason to stop time. Is this a premonition? Am I sensing the future?*

As Mrs. Sorenson answered her husband's query, he turned toward her for just a couple of seconds. That's all the time it took for a deer to jump from the trees at the road's edge and land in the road not more than twenty feet in front of their car.

"Look out!" she screamed. "Deer!"

Henri's thumbs closed on the stone from both sides and time stopped. Henri did not know how a car traveling forty-five miles per hour could suddenly freeze, but that's what happened. There was the deer staring right at them from a couple of feet in front of their car. They would have crashed into it if Henri hadn't stopped everything.

How did I know to do this? Henri wondered. *No time to think about that now. I must act.*

She unbuckled her seat belt. Carefully, she opened her door and got out. She approached the statuesque deer. She reached out and touched it. Frightened at the human touch, it bounded away across the road. Henri watched it disappear into the trees. She looked back the way the deer had come, and seeing no other deer, she returned to the car. She fastened her seat belt.

She thought for a moment, and then deciding there was nothing more she could do, she touched the stone again with both thumbs. As she did, the car sped through the space where the deer had been. They might have been killed if they had struck the deer.

She quickly put the necklace back inside her shirt.

"Where did he go?" shouted Mrs. Sorenson.

"How did we miss him?" questioned Mr. Sorenson. The car skidded to a stop in the middle of the road. His reflexes had caused him to hit the brakes. "Is everyone okay?" he asked in a shaky voice.

"Yes," replied all three at once. They had been wearing their seat belts so they were just a little shaken from the excitement.

Mr. Sorenson pulled the car completely off the road, and they all got out. They still had some water in the cooler in the trunk. Mr. Sorenson retrieved it and everyone had a big drink.

Just then three more deer came out of the woods behind them and crossed the road. It was just starting to get dark, but visibility was still very good.

"We sure were lucky," Erika said between gulps of water. "I was sure we were going to crash into that first deer. Did you see him, Henri?"

"Yes!" she replied. "I thought he had stopped right in front of us! He must have just bounded on across the road."

"I'm sure he stopped," Mrs. Sorenson added. "But if he did, why didn't we hit him?"

"Someone must be watching out for us," Erika's dad said. "Let's get on home. I've had enough excitement for one night."

"Me, too," Henri said. *And now I have another mystery I can't tell anyone about,* she thought.

Hank and Daryl had left the party earlier, so they were already safely home.

J.J., Mike, Jerry, Joey, and Mrs. Jamison had stayed a little longer to help Gramma Tessie clean up. It was about a half hour later when they left the party. Their trip home, like Daryl and Hank's, was uneventful.

Mr. Sorenson dropped Henri off at her house and then drove home. They arrived at eight o'clock just as it was getting completely dark. The days were getting longer signaling the beginning of summer.

And so ended the first week of summer vacation.

5

DR. EMORY WAS GOING TO BE VERY BUSY DURING THE NEXT two weeks. He would be an unbelievable distance from Earth. After he finished the meeting with Grams and Tessie, he went back to his house. He sat for a while, just thinking and wondering what he would find when he returned to Saros. He had been able to delay his departure until after school was out for the summer.

First, he had made contact with Grams and Tessie. They had been born on Earth many years ago. Besides raising families, they were learning about Earth people. They were part of the plan preparing for the birth of the one who would save the world of Saros and possibly even Earth.

Finally, he had been born. Even though he was still just a boy, he was now old enough for his training to begin. Dr. M would see to that. He would first need to learn from the situations as they presented themselves. His will and determination needed to be strengthened! J.J. Jamison had no idea how important he was to the universe! He would learn over time.

And that was the key element—time. As J.J. grew and matured, his powers would expand and grow stronger. He must learn to control them and to use them wisely.

The one whose birth was prophesied back on Saros many centuries ago was to be accompanied by another. She would be female, his partner in saving two worlds. It seemed that Tessie had found her also. Henri would also need to begin her training. Then the two would need to be told of the other's powers.

The old prophecies also said that this group would eventually number four. Dr. M wondered if Mike and Erika were the other two. *J.J.'s saving of Mike's life with the first use of his new power,* he thought, *lends credence to the idea that Mike is the one. Especially since Grams said she had been sure he was the one even before the accident took place. Now, Grams said she was positive. I must consult the prophecies back on Saros.*

Erika is still a mystery. There's nothing definitive that points to her as the fourth member of the team, he thought. *Time has a way of clarifying things.* "This will all work out so I can move forward," he finally said as he let his thoughts move toward his trip back to Saros.

Will the situation be even more unstable? Will the military still want to invade Earth? Will there be any improvement in the water situation? He was concerned about so many things. First, he would need to undergo forty-eight hours of cellular reconstruction at a secret facility as soon as he landed. Then he would get some answers.

A trip to the underground caverns of the mystics was also on his agenda. He needed to get two more of the precious Saros stones. If his calculations were correct, there were only two stones remaining. He hoped they were still safely hidden.

The ruling government on Saros will want to meet with me, he thought. *They will want an update on my progress on Earth.* Dr. M's thoughts wandered to the history of Saros. *It's a small planet, about the size of Mercury. It orbits a red sun at a distance of 90 million miles, about the same distance Earth is from its sun. The population numbers just under ten million. The people are divided in how they want to solve the water shortage situation. That's the big problem.*

He planned to stay on Saros for only two weeks. Hopefully, he would get everything done there that required his attention and get back to Earth quickly. He was sure someone had landed on Earth from Saros. There was nothing he could do about it right now. He had to return to Saros for treatment. Then he would deal with the situation here on Earth upon his return. Not too much could happen in two weeks, could it?

Another thought came into his mind. *I must work on the components for the magno-pulse. I will need to spend several hours in my lab. There must be a way to make it stronger and more effective. The small unit I brought here to Earth has worked quite well, but I am sure I can improve it. Then I will not have to keep making these trips back to Saros.*

Grams and Tessie have become undetectable as Saronians as are their offspring. Their children and grandchildren will never need to return to Saros for treatment. I must not let anyone from Saros learn that secret.

He could foresee needing a lot of help protecting Earth. He hoped the prophecy turned out to be completely true. J.J., Henri, Mike, and Erika were the key to everything.

6

HAROLD AND DALE AWOKE EARLY. THEY HAD BEEN ON Saros two years and four months. It was time to go home. They missed their families. The President of the United States had authorized their assignment here. It was an extraordinary attempt to try to both save a planet far away as well as prevent a possible invasion of Earth.

Major Stromberg had arranged to meet secretly with the two men back on Earth. Neither man wanted to leave his family. Upon learning the seriousness of the situation, the men decided they had no choice and agreed to help.

Harold and Dale were biochemical engineers as well as former marine officers. Both were amateur astronomers as well. They were well suited for the work they were recruited to do on Saros. They did not know that time was going to be a problem. The plan was for them to go to Saros and assist with the water treatment plans already underway there. They would also look at the advanced science of Saros to determine if there was a possible solution to the water problem. The original plan was for them to return to Earth within a year.

The ship from Saros had arrived on Earth from the dark side of the moon completely undetected. The men were picked up in the Siberian tundra and transported back to the moon. Within six hours the ship had left the moon using the space warp trans shield to enter the wormhole just outside the orbit of Pluto. The ship exited the wormhole 1.4 light-years from Earth. In two more hours, they would be on Saros.

Once on Saros, they met with the top scientists. They reviewed the water conservation methods currently in place. They made some improvements. If nothing changed, this would provide water for between twenty-five and thirty more years.

Next, they discussed and evaluated the water reclamation efforts being used on Blatos and Zinta, the two moons orbiting Saros. The water on these moons was frozen, and they wanted to thaw it and transport it to Saros.

After extensive testing, which took much longer than anticipated, the two Earth scientists determined that the water was poisoned with the chemical Stintonal. This was a deadly poison that had formed a chemical bond with the frozen water. There was no way they could be separated and the water made safe for consumption. The water there was useless.

The Saronian scientists knew that a new source of water needed to be found. Three generations ago, they had surveyed all planets up to half a light-year from Saros. No water had been found. During those explorations, they discovered the wormhole. After traveling through it, they discovered Earth. That Earth was nearly two-thirds water was the biggest discovery of all. Perhaps they could make a deal with Earth for some of its water. They could use that water.

One hundred years ago, a secret delegation had been dispatched to Earth. All members of the crew gathered information but learned too late about the effects of Earth's yellow sun on Saronians. After two months, all twenty-two members of the first delegation became ill and died. They did manage to send a message back to Saros explaining that they were sick and dying.

A friend of Dr. M's great-grandfather came on the second ship to Earth. He was a scientist and came with a crew of ten. They gathered more information and returned to Saros after one month. Their conclusion was that the yellow sun caused the Saronian cellular structure to degenerate. They could stay just under two months, but would need special treatment immediately upon returning to Saros.

These first explorers started to work on a treatment to protect them from the rays of the Earth's sun. It was J.J.'s great-grandfather who finally isolated the cellular component that started him on the right research leading to a solution.

Wanting to test his hypothesis, he convinced the government to send a delegation of scientists to Earth. This group included ten specialized researchers. There were five married couples.

J.J.'s great-grandfather was the lead scientist. One of the scientists was his distant cousin who made the trip because of his military and security training.

After two months, they were still alive but very weak. Their research finally led them to develop a partial solution that kept them alive.

Three of the wives were biophysicists. Dr. Jamison's wife helped him modify his pulsator enough so that it protected and prolonged their lives. As they gained strength, they knew they were on the right path.

They used their scientific knowledge to get jobs at a research facility in England. As they learned more about Earth, they wanted to work around fresh water. Fortunately, they were able to transfer to jobs in the Great Lakes area.

They kept in touch with Saros but never fully regained their health. They sent their research back to the scientists on Saros who continued their work. A controllable solution was never found.

Four of the couples had children while living on Earth. The children seemed immune to the yellow sun's effects their parents had experienced. However, there was a slight degeneration of their cellular structure that became evident after the age of fifty.

Meanwhile, the water situation on Saros was getting worse. Finally, two generations later, Dr. M was sent to Earth. He would secretly meet with government contacts the previous

Saronians had made. Because of his extensive knowledge about space, much of which he kept secret, he obtained a job with the government as an expert UFO researcher. This was how he got involved with the military base in New Mexico. His cover had been set up as an elementary teacher.

When Dr. M was contacted about going to Earth, he did research regarding the previous ventures there. He learned, with the help of some government officials, that it was his great-grandfather and a distant cousin who had gone to Earth to try to solve the cellular degeneration problem. That was when he discovered that his grandfather had been working on a new pulse machine that altered the cellular structure of Saronians. This made them less susceptible to the damaging yellow rays of Earth's sun.

He was saddened to learn that six of these brave scientists had eventually died from the effects of the yellow sun shortly after reaching age fifty. Records also indicated that J.J.'s grandfather had sent his research back to Saros. After discovering this, Dr. M decided he would dedicate his life to finding a solution to this problem. He would continue that research. With some difficulty, he obtained the scientific papers from the sealed archives.

Some of the records of the original group of scientists had been lost. All of the families had stayed close together except Gramma Tessie's niece. She had moved away and lost contact with the group.

Several years later and after many trips back to Saros, Dr. M discovered a partial solution. He was ready to try to perfect this latest improvement. This could be the one. It would make it possible for Saronians to stay on Earth for up to ten years.

Through his government contacts, Dr. M finally met Major Stromberg. Together they had meetings with several governments. No one except the United States took them seriously. The other countries thought they were crazy or simply said they would fight if anyone tried to take any of Earth's water. Working with the U.S. president had proved to be beneficial. They concluded there was no way Earth's inhabitants would allow another planet to take even a little bit of the water on Earth.

Dr. M also did some research and study with the mystical elders in the underground caves of Saros. It was there that he had learned of the doom facing his planet with the water shortage and the prophesied birth of one very special and powerful person on a planet far away who would play a primary role in the conflict between two planets.

Then the unthinkable happened. The underground military on Saros learned about Earth and the abundant water supply there. Immediately plans started to be made for an invasion.

Dr. M's discovery of the magno-pulse was indeed the breakthrough he thought it might be. It also represented a potentially dangerous cure. The underground must never find out about his discovery. If they obtained it, there would be war with Earth. The result could contaminate both the Earth and its water supply. He could not let that happen.

The opposition underground was not in favor of asking for Earth's help. They wanted to invade Earth, take over the planet, and send millions of Saronians there to live. Eventually they wanted all ten million of Saros' inhabitants to move to Earth and abandon Saros. This political group had the backing of a small but well-equipped military unit. They were living on one of the few habitable land masses on Saros. They also had control of eleven spacecraft capable of making the trip to Earth. The government in power had control of twenty such spacecraft.

. . . .

The opposition had been trying to obtain the formula for Dr. M's special antidote, the magno-pulse, for some time now. Thus far they have been unsuccessful. The conversation at their military headquarters currently centered on that topic.

"Captain Stamtu," called out Colonel Jabu. "Have you made any progress in obtaining the magno-pulse formula?"

"No, Colonel. I've tried everything I can think of. Dr. M is due to return for his rejuvenation treatment. Perhaps we can intercept and kidnap him."

"I'll consider that, but I'm sure the government would sacrifice his life to keep the formula safe from us. We don't know where the formula is or even who knows where it is kept. The last person we bribed on the Council mysteriously disappeared right after we paid her. We are attempting to contact another council member."

Little did they know that Dr. Emory soon would not need to return to Saros for treatment every few months. He had previously developed a formula that would let him to stay on Earth up to two years. He had kept coming back every three months just to keep the opposition from learning the truth. Now he was returning because of his need for the Saros stones to help fulfill the prophecy. He also had an idea for greatly improving the magno-pulse that could only be done in his lab on Saros.

"Should we move forward with the invasion plan, Colonel?"

"Yes. I want more research done on the weapons. We need them tested on Earth. I plan to send ten soldiers and three diplomats to Earth in three to four months.

"Continue with the infiltration training. Everyone must be versed in Earth's customs and language. We want to land and blend in with the population.

"The goal of this mission will be to ascertain where to land the invasion force, work to find ways to cripple Earth's defenses, and to test new weapons.

"I plan to send the invasion force to Earth in eight to nine months. We'll continue working on the formula angle in hopes of a breakthrough before we launch. If we cannot get the magno-pulse formula, then we'll just send replacements every two months. That will be a real hardship, but I think we can make it work. Maybe we will even have our own formula by then."

. . . .

Dale and Harold were meeting with Commander Tammer. "How are you dealing with the opposition and their insistence on invading Earth?" Dale asked.

"We have infiltrated their ranks with two of our best operatives. We think one of them will be sent with their first ship to Earth. He just reported to us that one ship will be sent with thirteen people on board. If we are lucky enough for him to be included, then he can sabotage their efforts once they get to Earth," he replied.

"How will he identify the Saronians if they change their shape to look like the Earthlings?"

"We have supplied him with a modified Saros crystal that blends with his body. It will help locate and identify our people. It is undetectable. We just have to hope he is included with that first group."

"What more can we do here?" Harold wanted to know.

"Do you have any more ideas regarding our water problem?"

"Yes," replied Dale this time. "We've studied your technology and spoken with many of your top scientists. We have another idea we'd like to try. It will take some time, and we need you to get us back to our own solar system to test it."

"Of course. What do you need?"

"We need to be taken to Neptune and Uranus, two of the more distant planets from Earth's sun. We studied them before we left, and we think there might be enough frozen water there to sustain your planet for many Earth years. We have modified some of your advanced equipment, which will allow us to analyze the ice once we get there."

"Are you sure about this?"

"No, but it's the most promising plan we've developed. We'll have to do some more tests on the planets. That will take about a week after we arrive there. Can you get us there?" Dale inquired.

"We sure can!" the commander excitedly responded. "This could solve our problem long enough for us to find a permanent solution."

"Yes, but will it satisfy those here who want to invade Earth?" Harold asked.

"I don't know. I will try to contact them and see. They might not believe us. They might still want to invade your planet as a backup plan. I won't know until I talk with them. I will initiate a contact right away."

"Then let's make plans to get us to Neptune. After we complete the studies there, can you return us to Earth? We'd like to see our families again. We weren't allowed to even say goodbye to them. We just disappeared."

"Yes, we will be happy to do that for you. And you will have our profound thanks if this plan of yours works. We'll start to prepare the ships for your return immediately. They should be ready to depart in four days."

7

DEEP IN THE WOODS IN AN OLD ABANDONED CABIN A FEW miles from Gramma Tessie's house, three unsavory characters were gathered. "Does the High Council know we are here?" Dagnaut asked.

"No, I do not think so," replied Joblanc. "I was able to use the same space warp trans shield Dr. M used when he came here the last time. Then our trip from the moon near the fifth planet from their sun was made using the phantom ship we were given by the Saros military. The bad luck came when we lost power and crashed in what the Earth people call Siberia. It was very unfortunate that those people had to see us crash. Hopefully, the Earthlings will never figure out what really happened there."

"How long can we safely stay here?" Zolar asked.

"We can only stay two months. We have not been treated with the magno-pulse Dr. M has secretly developed. That is how he stays here for so long," explained Dagnaut.

"Our locating crystal brought us here. That is how we found him. Next, we have to find out what he is planning," continued Zolar.

"What I do not understand is the part the old lady plays in all this," Dagnaut stated. "I saw the boat coming across the lake, so I spied on them. I think I heard her mention the Stone of Saros. How could she have one of those powerful stones? Our detector that locates native Saronians did not register her as one," explained Dagnaut. "We will have to watch her."

"Did you see the stone?" asked Zolar.

"No," answered Dagnaut. "But she did give the girl something and said it had special powers. She said the girl was the next one who could use its powers. She also mentioned something about it being important to the future."

"Did you hear anything else?" questioned Zolar.

"No," replied Dagnaut. "I was too far away to hear everything. I think the girl put something around her neck, but she had her back to me the entire time."

"I think we should watch the girl, too," Joblanc suggested.

"That is a good idea," added Zolar. "Maybe we should put recording modules in her house."

"No, I do not think so," Joblanc said. "She is just a kid and poses no threat to our mission. We will follow her once in a while or try to listen when she comes to Tessie's house. Maybe we will hear something useful. We should consider searching her room if we can determine a time when no one will be home. We might find the stone her grandmother gave her. We will drive past once in a while to look over the place. If the opportunity presents itself, we will steal the stone. Then we can discover if it is real or not."

"Enough talking about these other people. What about us?" Zolar asked with a worried look on his face. "Because our ship crashed, how will we get back to Saros in two months before we die from exposure to the yellow sun?"

"We saved our communication devices. We can try to contact our base on the moon near the fifth planet and tell them our situation. But our mission is still on. We must gather information on Dr. M and try to discover what his mission here is. Then we can report it back to our base," Dagnaut stated.

"We must set up surveillance on his house. We also need to get inside and install listening devices and recording modules," said Joblanc, his golden features turning a bright shade of yellow. "We do not have much time. The colonel thinks his mission has something to do with stopping our planned invasion."

"If we could get that secret formula for the magno-pulse, we could move the invasion up much sooner," grumbled Dagnaut. "It will not do much good to invade if we have to return to Saros every two months."

"The colonel is working on that back on Saros," stated Zolar. "The secret must be there because Dr. M keeps returning there."

"First, we must communicate with our base. What do they call that planet where we landed?" Dagnaut asked.

"Jupiter, I think. We chose it because it is so large. We were able to hide our small base easily on one of its moons," Joblanc stated matter-of-factly. "The Earthlings do not know we are here, so they certainly won't be looking for us."

"Do they believe they are the only intelligent beings in the universe?" Zolar questioned.

"Yes, they do," responded Dagnaut. "That little misconception is going to cost them. Our attack will be a big surprise. When they figure out what is happening, it will be too late. We will already control their planet."

"Only if everything goes as our leaders are planning," Zolar added. "You know that never happens. Something either goes wrong or a surprise pops up. Look at what should have been a smooth flight and landing on Earth. Now, because of our crash, we might be stranded here to die from yellow sun poisoning." He started to complain some more when Dagnaut interrupted him.

"Stop that! There will be no complaining. We must work together and make our mission a success. That is the part we play. Our information will help the general to plan the invasion," Dagnaut continued. "We must determine exactly where the invasion force would land. Earth is a big planet and our troops must gain control quickly as they will be greatly outnumbered. Strategic landings will be very important."

Joblanc spoke next. "We must get some Earth currency and purchase a computer. We can use it in connection with the one we brought from Saros. If we can connect to their internet, we can search all over the world. Then we can relay what we learn to our leaders back on Saros."

"I was able to save the sonic vibrator and the duo-replicator from the crash," Zolar said. "I think we can replicate their currency without any problem."

"Good," Joblanc said with finality. "Then we should go inside and start to work. Zolar, you and Dagnaut get the electronic equipment ready. I would like to get it in place tomorrow when no one is home. I am quite sure Dr. M just went back to Saros. I will contact our base to ask about that and our rescue. Tessie usually goes into town for groceries on a regular schedule. We will go in when she leaves her house. It will take us less than an hour to get the equipment set up. She is usually gone much longer than that. I followed her last week, and she stopped to eat lunch and was gone for three hours."

"That sounds like a great plan," Zolar added. "The general wants information from us as fast as we can gather it. We had better get to work."

"Do we have enough food?" Dagnaut wanted to know.

"No," Joblanc responded. "We will need to use some of the currency Zolar is going to replicate. Then we can go into town and get everything we need. We must stay out of town and out of sight as much as possible. We do not want to arouse any suspicions regarding our presence here.

"This cabin is in really bad shape. I doubt anyone ever comes near it. It will be the perfect place to stay while we complete our mission," Joblanc went on. "Once we clean it up, the place will be habitable. We will not make any fires. No sense drawing attention to the place. We will complete our work and be gone before anyone knows we are here."

They received confirmation that Dr. M was indeed on his way to Saros. So that evening they drove to Dr. M's house. They parked on the street and walked to the front door, carrying two briefcases. It was just after dark, and the porch light was on as well as a lamp in the front window.

"I will knock to be sure no one is inside," Zolar said.

"Good idea," Dagnaut replied. "He might have a house sitter."

When no one answered, the three calmly walked around the side of the house. There were tall bushes there between Dr. M's house and his neighbor. They found an unlocked window on the back of the house. Soon all three were inside.

"You two check the kitchen. I will check the next room," Dagnaut ordered. "Search his cabinets and decide where to put the recorder."

After a quick search, Joblanc shouted out, "Look what I found: two one-hundred-dollar bills, three twenties, a five, and six ones in the cookie jar inside a cupboard."

"I can use them in the replicator to make more U.S. currency," Zolar said with a satisfied smile.

They joined Dagnaut in the next room to decide where to put the first recorder.

"I think we should put one inside that register in the wall," Joblanc suggested.

"I will do that," Zolar said as he got a chair to stand on and pulled out a screwdriver to remove the vent cover.

"Joblanc, look around the other rooms and see if he has an office," ordered Dagnaut again.

Zolar was finished installing the first recorder when Joblanc returned. "No office," he reported. "Just three bedrooms and two bathrooms."

"Then we will put the other recorder in the ceiling vent in the kitchen. Aim it at the table, Zolar," Dagnaut stated with authority. He seemed to be in charge.

"When did you say Dr. M was returning from Saros?" Zolar asked.

"Not for a couple of weeks," answered Dagnaut. "Get that last recorder installed so we can get out of here. Then we can safely listen to Dr. M from half a mile away. Hopefully, he will say something that will tell us what his plans are. General Blubick is counting on us. We might get a promotion if we do well on this assignment."

"That would be great!" Zolar concluded.

They finished their work and left through the same back window where they had entered. Slowly, they walked around the side of the house and out to the street. No one saw them as they got into their car and drove away.

"Dr. M will never know we were in his house. Good job, men," Dagnuat congratulated his team.

They were in for a surprise when Dr. M returned home.

Zolar was successful in replicating the Earth currency. He made them a little over $200,000. He made a lot of one hundred dollar bills. He also made several thousand dollars in twenties and fives. When they finished duplicating the money, they returned it.

"There is a small used car dealership on the edge of Millville," Dagnaut said. "Tomorrow we will go there and buy a car. Then we can get rid of this car we 'borrowed' from that old junkyard on our way here."

"We can also buy some food and a computer," added Joblanc.

The next day was Tessie's grocery shopping day. The three spies were driving about a mile from Tessie's house when she passed them going in the direction of town.

"This is our chance to put the listening devices in her house," Joblanc said.

"Do you have everything we need?" Dagnaut asked.

"Yes," Zolar replied.

It only took forty-five minutes to complete the installation. Now everything said at Tessie's house would be recorded.

8

AT NOON, FIVE DAYS AFTER DR. M HAD LEFT FOR SAROS, Grams got a message from him. He had left her an intergalactic communications device developed on Saros. It only took ten hours for the message to go between the two planets. The signal was sent from Saros to a communications station at the edge of the wormhole. Then the message was relayed through the wormhole to a station at the other end. From there, the message was sent on to Earth where Grams received it:

"Grams, contact Tess and meet with her. Things are bad on Saros. An invasion of Earth could come in the next year. Plan to get J.J. and Henri together. Give them all the information you think they need. They will need to start building a bond with each other. Meet at your house. Contact Tess in person. Do not call her. Three Saros military men have landed on Earth and may have located me in Millville before I left. Be careful!"

Grams nearly collapsed. "I should be sitting down when hearing things like this," she shuddered. Her hands were shaking and her knees felt weak. Quickly, she plunked herself down in an easy chair. After several relaxing deep breaths, she considered what to do. She would drive over to Tess's house right away and invite her out to the farm. She would think of some excuse to get her there. Dr. M must think it unsafe to talk at Tess's place.

Now, she must determine what to tell J.J. and Henri. She and Tess could talk about that. Things would need to move along much faster with the training of these kids. At ages twelve and thirteen, they could be thrust into a planet-wide war. This made her worry even more. She spent the next hour thinking and planning what to tell Tess about the meeting and what they must talk about. This would be a crucial meeting.

Grams finally got up and went into her bedroom. She changed into going out clothes. She usually wore comfortable old things around the farm. Going into town required that she look a little nicer. She decided to get some groceries after a quick stop at Tess's place. This was a good reason for being in town.

Grams decided to skirt the town on her way to Tess's house. She drove a couple of extra miles north, so when she turned east, she was already north of town. It only took twenty minutes to get there.

There was no sign of Tess's Tahoe, but it could be in the garage. After parking in the driveway, she walked to the front door. When Tess did not answer after several knocks, Grams thought to herself, *I hope nothing has happened to Tess.*

Could those soldiers have found out about her? Shaking these thoughts aside, she walked around the house to the backyard. There was Tess sitting at a table down by the lake. Her head was bowed down and a hat was pulled over her face. *Oh, no!* she thought. *What's happened to Tess?*

"Hey, Tess," she called out tentatively while looking all around the big yard.

"Hi, Grams," Tess yawned and got up. "I was taking a little siesta. What brings you out here?"

"You don't need to get up. I'll just be here a few minutes."

Tess slowly sat back down. "What's the hurry? Sit and talk a while."

Grams came next to Tess, leaned near her face, and softly whispered, "Meet me at my house at ten o'clock tomorrow morning. I have heard from Dr. M. We have to talk privately and make some plans. Don't say anything about this now. He thinks someone from Saros has landed on Earth. If they have located him, they could be nearby. The only safe place to talk is at my house."

"Okay," she whispered back. "I'll be there." In a louder normal voice Tess continued, "Can you come inside for a lemonade? It's quite warm today."

"Sure. That sounds good. It will refresh me before I continue into town. I need to purchase some groceries. The kids have been out a couple of times, and I'm running low on food supplies."

"Those young kids sure can eat, can't they?"

"That's for sure."

They walked back to the house and went inside. Zolar and Joblanc had been hiding in the trees and bushes in the lot next door. They heard Grams' greeting but had not noticed the whispers.

"It looks like a social call," Zolar stated. "Nothing to worry about. Do you think we should get closer and try to listen?"

"No. The recording module will get everything they say inside. We will retrieve the recording electronically after dark tonight," Joblanc said. "Then we will decide if we need to start listening to Grams' conversations." They sneaked back through the trees to their car and drove to the cabin where they were hiding.

Once inside the house, the two ladies had a normal conversation. Grams drank a glass of lemonade while sitting in the front room with Tess. They talked about food, TV, the weather, and family. Nothing sounded out of the ordinary. There would be no clues for the spies.

Half an hour later, Grams commented, "I guess I had better be going now. The grocery store will get busy if I shop too late in the day."

"I think you will be early enough to beat the crowd," Tess replied. "Come out anytime."

"Thanks. I'll do that. Would you like to play dominoes some time?"

"Sure, I love that game."

"So do I."

"Let me think. Today is Tuesday. Could you come back on Friday? I'll make some sandwiches, and we can play dominoes down by the lake."

"That will be great. I'll be here at noon." The two ladies got up and walked out to Grams' car.

As Grams drove away, a serious look came across Tess's face. *I wonder how serious the situation is,* she thought. *It must be real trouble if we have to meet secretly at Grams' farm.*

Grams made an uneventful stop at the grocery store in town. She also stopped at the card shop and the gas station before heading back to the farm. She arrived home a little after four o'clock. She spent the next hour sitting on the front porch thinking about what she and Tess needed to talk about. She also thought a lot about the kids and planned a way to get Henri and J.J. together at the farm. *Dr. M said it was time for them to know about each other,* she thought to herself. *This will be a delicate situation. Should I reveal our true identities? Should I let them see us as we really are? I'll need to sleep on this. Perhaps tomorrow will bring more clarity,* she decided.

The next day, Tess took a circuitous route to Grams' farm. She went a way she had never traveled before. She also turned on the anti-tracking device Dr. M had given her. It fastened into the far back top in the trunk of her car. It was invisible and made no sounds. It made her car electronically invisible.

She arrived at Grams' farm at 9:55 a.m. She had made several stops and backtracked three times and was sure no one was following her. She was right.

9

SUMMER VACATION WAS ONLY TWO WEEKS OLD, AND ALREADY Mike was bored. He had not seen nor talked with J.J. in over a week. An idea came to him, and within a few seconds he was calling J.J.

"Hello," answered J.J.

"Hi, buddy," Mike replied. "What're you doing?"

"Nothing much. I've read a little but that's about it. Anything exciting happening with you?"

"No, I'm just bored. I hate to say it, but I would be okay if school started tomorrow."

"Hey! I'm not that bored yet. Come on over, and we'll see if we can think of something to do."

"Okay," Mike replied and hung up the phone. He wondered if he should take anything with him to J.J.'s house. "Nah. I don't know what to take anyway," he said to no one.

Mike took the backyard shortcut. He was almost to J.J.'s when he heard a loud, hysterical scream coming from the small house next to J.J.'s place. He slowed and stopped at the edge of the tree line. There were some big bushes there, so he pushed them aside slowly and peeked through. The back of Mrs. Montague's house was thirty feet away. He saw two men push Mrs. Montague back into the house. One of the men had a gun.

"Get back inside, you old goat," the man with the gun said. "If you want to stay alive, you'll open the floor safe right now. Otherwise, this house will need a new tenant."

"I don't have a floor safe," she stated. "Where did you get that idea? I don't even have any valuables to put inside a safe. I don't understand this," she cried. Big wet tears started down her eighty-five-year-old cheeks. "I have no money or valuables. Please leave me alone," she begged.

"Shut up and quit your blubbering! Jeb, get the rope from the bag we brought in. We'll tie her up and then ransack the house. There must be valuables here somewhere," Boyd said.

"Come on, Boyd. Why do I have to do all the work?" Jeb complained. "You're not the boss, you know."

"Hey, who planned this caper?"

"I guess you did."

"Then that makes me the boss. Get her tied up."

Mike had crept from bush to bush and finally stopped ten feet from the back door of the house. He did not know what to do. *I don't want to get shot. These guys sound mean,* he thought to himself. He decided to sneak over to J.J.'s house. Upon safely reaching it, he rushed right in. J.J., Jerry, and their mom were sitting at the dining room table on the far side of the house, talking.

"Sorry to barge in. I just saw a man with a gun push Mrs. Montague through the back door into her house. I didn't know what to do. He was yelling at her to open her floor safe if she wanted to stay alive."

"Let's call 9-1-1 first," Mrs. Jamison said. She dialed the number and handed the phone to Mike. He calmly told the operator what he had seen.

"I've dispatched three units. They should be there within four minutes," the dispatcher told Mike. "You and anyone else there stay inside. Do not try to stop them if they come outside."

"Oh!" shouted J.J. "They're outside. Poor Mrs. Montague is being forced into the backseat of the car with one of the robbers. It looks like they are kidnapping her! The other one is getting into the front seat. What should we do? They're getting away!"

"Stay inside. Give me a description of the car they're driving. Do not try to stop them. The officers should be there any minute."

The officers did not arrive in time. The car drove away to the west and out of town. The police cruisers arrived three minutes after the kidnappers left.

"Which way did they go?" Sergeant Mills demanded. "What kind of car were they driving? Did you get the plate number?"

J.J. replied, a little shaken, "The car was a newer Dodge, a Durango, I think. It was jet black with dark-tinted windows. The lady on the phone from 9-1-1 told us to stay inside, so we didn't get the plate number. I can tell you that it is a Michigan plate, but that's all. They drove west very fast."

Sergeant Mills gave orders to the other two officers there with him. "Stan and Nick. You go after the suspects. I'll call the highway patrol and the state police. Then I'll check the house."

"Okay, Sergeant," replied Officer Cole. He and Officer Jones quickly got into their patrol cars and started in pursuit.

After a careful search of the house, Sergeant Mills came back outside. "There's nothing helpful on the inside. Do you have any idea what the robbers were after, J.J.?"

"Actually, it was Mike who first spotted them. He heard them yelling at Mrs. Montague," explained J.J.

"I was coming over to see J.J. when I heard a loud, angry voice. I stopped at the edge of the trees and saw a man with a gun. He and an accomplice pushed Mrs. Montague back inside her house through the back door. The man with the gun was asking her where her floor safe was. That's all I heard. Then I went to J.J.'s house to ask him what we should do. His mom had me call 9-1-1."

"Can you describe the robbers?"

"Somewhat. I was so scared for Mrs. Montague that I concentrated on her more than the robbers. Let's see. One of the kidnappers was five or six inches taller than the other. I would put him at about 160 to 175 pounds. He was sort of stocky. His hair was black. It looked short, but he had a Detroit Tiger's baseball cap on. He had on tight blue jeans and a plain dark blue sweatshirt. That's all I can remember."

"We'll get the police artist out here and you can work up a sketch. You did a good job. If there is no floor safe, then they must have decided to kidnap her. There could be a ransom call coming in soon. I'll get the department to send out a sketch artist, and we'll put a wire tap on her phone and yours.

"I will authorize the department to send a man out to spend the night in the house next door. If a call comes in, we'll let you know."

"Thanks. We're the only family Mrs. Montague has in town," Mrs. Jamison said. "We'll do whatever it takes to get her back safely."

"That might be what the kidnappers are counting on," replied Sergeant Mills. "That's all we can do for now. Let's hope Nick and Stan were able to locate the getaway car and rescue Mrs. Montague. The state police will set up roadblocks. Perhaps they'll catch the kidnappers. Otherwise, I'll be back in the morning." With that Sergeant Mills walked over to his patrol car and left.

About twenty minutes later, two big black sedans and a white panel truck with police markings on the side arrived at the scene. These were the forensics specialists and the detectives. These people would dust for fingerprints and look for anything the robbers might have left behind.

The detectives came over to J.J.'s house. When J.J. answered the doorbell, he was greeted by three men, each wearing a black suit. "Good evening, young man. I'm Detective Sampson. These men are Detective Smathers and Detective Smith. We would like to ask the witness a few questions. Is Mike here?"

"Yes. He's here. He's best friends with my son," Mrs. Jamison explained as she came to the door.

"May we speak with him, please?"

"Sure," replied Mike as he entered the room. "What would you like to know?"

"Tell us everything you saw and heard," ordered the tallest of the detectives. He must have been six feet four inches tall with broad shoulders. He cut quite an intimidating figure as he towered over everyone.

Mike repeated the story he had told Sergeant Mills earlier. The detectives only asked one question after they listened to what Mike had to say. Then Detective Smith spoke up. "Are you sure there were just two of them?"

"Yes. I got a good look at one of the guys." He repeated the same description he had given Sergeant Mills.

Then the questions started coming faster. "Did he have any scars or tattoos?"

"None that I could see. Wait a minute. I was quite a distance away, but I remember the man's gun hand looked very red. That might have been a tattoo. There was also some type of tattoo on the back of his neck on the right side. He held the gun in his left hand, so he must have been left-handed. That's the hand with the red spot."

"Did you see anything else when they got into the car to make their getaway?"

"I did," Mrs. Jamison tentatively spoke up. "There were only two of them. It happened so fast that I don't remember very much. But now that I think back, I can picture them coming out of the house and forcing Mrs. Montague into the back of their car. They seemed to be arguing and waving their arms at each other.

"One of the kidnappers was a little taller than the other. He opened the car door while the other pushed her inside. They weren't very gentle, considering she is quite elderly. Each of them was much taller than Mrs. Montague. One was five eight or five nine and weighed one hundred sixty to one seventy. He had very dark hair sticking out from under a Detroit Tigers baseball cap like Mike said. The other was five or six inches taller. He seemed to be in charge. His hair was brown. It was kind of fluffy and hung down to his shoulders. He was wearing dark sunglasses. His shirt was dark green with some kind of dark circles on the back. He also had on jeans. That's all I can remember."

"That's good work. Although you have given us a lot of information, it does not narrow the search much. This will take some time, but we'll get them. I think that's all for now. If you remember anything else, please call me. Here's my card. Thanks."

Forty-five minutes after the attempted robbery and the kidnapping, the neighborhood again was very quiet.

"What should we do now?" Mike wanted to know.

"I think we should stay here at my house," J.J. replied. "Then we'll be close if the police learn anything."

"Want me to order a large pizza?" Mrs. Jamison asked.

"Good idea," Mike said with a big smile. He was always hungry. "Anyone want to shoot some hoops?"

"Sure," J.J. replied. "I need to do something physical to get my mind off Mrs. Montague." He went into the garage and brought out the basketball. There was a hoop on the garage. They shot baskets and played H-O-R-S-E for about half an hour.

When the pizza arrived, they moved to the porch where they sat eating pizza and drinking pop for another half hour. It was still light out even at seven o'clock on this cool summer evening. The sun had just gone below the horizon, but the western sky was still ablaze with a brilliant pink and purple glow.

As the sun was sinking, so were J.J.'s hopes for Mrs. Montague. He wanted to do something. *I didn't know how long the robbers had been at Mrs. Montague's house,* he thought. *But I didn't even think about resetting time to try to protect her. What could I have done against a gun?* He felt guilty for not trying.

Mike interrupted J.J.'s thoughts with his own lament. "I just stood there hiding in the trees. I should have done something to try to stop them."

"You couldn't do anything, Mike. The man had a gun. You didn't know how many more guys were inside the house. Coming here to call 9-1-1 was the best thing to do. I'm just thinking like you. I wish I could've done more."

"What do you think the robbers will want?" Mike wanted to know. "She isn't rich, is she?"

"No," J.J. replied, "but I can see how someone might think so. Even though her house is very small, she keeps it in excellent condition. Her landscaping and flowers are beautiful. Even though she's quite elderly, she keeps herself in good shape. She was a natural blond and keeps her hair styled and dyed blond. She dresses conservatively but always looks like she is dressed for a night on the town. Her Cadillac is ten years old, but it still looks nearly new. She's such a pleasant lady. I hope they don't hurt her."

Just then two police cruisers pulled up and parked on the street. One officer went into the house next door. The other one came directly to J.J.'s house. "Is Mrs. Jamison here?" Officer Cole asked. "We have some new information."

Mrs. Jamison had seen the cars pull up, so she was coming through the double doors onto the large porch. "Here I am. What's happened?"

"Nothing exciting, I'm afraid. I wanted to let you know we found the kidnappers' car. It was stolen from Hartford ten miles north of here. We found it parked in a farm supply warehouse parking lot. They must have had another car waiting. We looked at the surveillance tapes of the parking lot, but the area where the car was didn't appear on the video. So we're at a dead end for now. We put out a BOLO (be on the lookout) across the state, but now, all we can do is wait."

"Did anyone at the warehouse see anything?" asked Mrs. Jamison.

"No. The place does most of its business early mornings and Saturdays. There was only one car in the lot when we were there. The employee said there had been no customers since around four o'clock. He was closing up when we arrived."

"I'm so worried," Mrs. Jamison said. "Is there anything we can do?"

"No. Don't worry. Something will turn up," Officer Cole stated as he went next door to help examine the crime scene again.

10

ERIKA WAS ADMIRING THE GORGEOUS WESTERN SKY AS SHE got to Deano's. The seven-block walk was easy to make with the beautiful summer weather they had been having. She was thinking about getting a banana split.

Henri had called an hour earlier and suggested ice cream. They were meeting at Deano's.

There were eight or so kids at the hangout when she arrived. Hank greeted her as she came through the door. "Hi, Erika. It's nice to see you. Looks like you get your pick of seats today." He flashed his biggest and brightest smile at her.

"Hi, Hank. It's good to see you, too. Are you always here working? Every time I come in you're here. Don't you have a life outside of Deano's?"

"Sure. I only work late afternoons and evenings Wednesday through Saturday. I get Sunday, Monday, and Tuesday off." As he turned to look around, he saw his boss coming. "Uh-oh, here comes the boss. I need to keep moving. Nice talking with you."

"Same here," responded Erika.

"Hey, Erika. What's up?" called a boy sitting with two other boys and a girl in a nearby booth. "Come on over."

"Hi, Chuck. Who are your friends?"

"This is Ann, Freddie, and Bill. Ann and Freddie are brother and sister visiting from Canada. Bill has been in my class at school the past three years. We're best friends."

"Hi, everyone. Great to meet you all."

"Same here," they all replied.

"What brings you two to Millville?"

"We're visiting our grandmother out at the lake for the summer. So far we're rather bored. Bill's uncle owns the house next to our grandmother's on the lake. We met Bill and Chuck out there."

"Which lake are you staying at?" Erika wanted to know.

"I think it's called Heart Lake. It's just a little north of town," Ann smiled at this interest in where she was staying.

"This is amazing!" Erika replied with growing enthusiasm. "My best friend's grandmother has a house on that same lake. We go there all the time to swim and hang out. Maybe we could meet you there sometime."

"That would be great! I don't know any girls here. It would be fun to have someone to talk girl talk with. Don't get me wrong. My brother, Freddie, is a great little brother, and Bill and Chuck are great guys. But they're boys. Get it?"

"I sure do. Write down your telephone number, and I'll call you tomorrow after I tell Henri all about you guys."

Ann wrote her number on a napkin and handed it to Erika. Ann was finally happy to be in Millville. Up to that point, it had been a miserable two weeks.

Erika said goodbye and walked up to the bar stools. By now, all the booths were taken. She sat down on one of the stools. There were only three open.

"Hi, Erika," came a familiar voice.

"Oh, hi, Bob. Are you working today?" Bob is two grades ahead of Erika, and they met last year when Erika took an advanced math class that Bob was in.

"Yes, but only a little longer. Then it's off to the drag races with my uncle. He's racing his old car again. He finished first in his class two weeks ago."

"Have fun. Those cars are very noisy. And the smoke from the tires when they burn rubber smells awful."

"I guess you just have to get used to it. I don't notice it at all anymore. Erika, would you like to go see a movie with me the day after tomorrow?"

"Wow. This is kind of sudden, Bob. I didn't know you liked me."

"I've been wanting to ask you out for a long time. What do you say? Would you go to the matinee with me Sunday? There are three shows that start at one thirty, two thirty, and three o'clock. You can take your pick."

"Yes, I'd like to go with you. What are the shows?"

Bob couldn't stop smiling. He was positively beaming. The prettiest girl in the school had just agreed to go on a date with him. "I don't know much about the movies, but there's quite a variety. *Mystery at the Big Top, Big Sister Trouble,* and *The Ride of Your Life* in 3-D are the best of what's showing. I think the first one is about an accident on the high wire when someone gets killed. They suspect foul play and call in a big name investigator to work the case. The second is about a fourteen-year-old who doesn't get along with her meddling eighteen-year-old sister. It doesn't sound very good. The third is a documentary showing plant and fish life around a reef, as well as big game up close in Africa. What do you think?"

"I like the first one and the last one. Let's ask around and see if anyone has seen them. I have to ask my parents if I can go. Then we can decide tomorrow. Is that all right with you?"

"It sure is. I've got to keep waiting on customers. I'll call you tomorrow before I come in to work. I start at three o'clock and work until ten."

"Okay." Erika hadn't noticed Henri come in and stand nearby listening. It was not a large place, so she had little choice but to stand and wait.

"Well," Henri smirked, "what have we here? A little summer romance budding?"

"It's just a movie date, Henri. Don't get excited about it. Bob is a great looking guy. He's really friendly and everyone likes him. Let's take this one step at a time."

"I see. You're just experimenting with this dating stuff."

"I'm only in seventh grade after all. It's a little early to get serious about anyone. We'll just see a movie, talk, and eat some popcorn."

"That sounds harmless enough. How are you getting to the movie?" Henri asked.

"Bob only lives five blocks away, and the theater is between his house and mine. So I guess he will walk to my house, and then we'll walk to the theater. I'm sure my parents will approve. After all, it's a daytime date."

"I'm sure you will have fun. What movie do you plan to see?"

"Bob mentioned three. Two sounded fairly good. One is a 3-D documentary that should have some spectacular color in it. The other is a mystery with a circus setting. Either one will be fine with me. Maybe sometime you could get a date and the four of us could go to a movie."

"No way, Erika. I want nothing to do with boys. I'm friends with Mike and J.J. That's enough to last me through high school."

"Oh, you'll change your mind someday, Henri. I know you will," Erika encouraged.

"Don't hold your breath," laughed Henri.

"Look. A booth just opened. Let's take it," Erika said as she made a beeline for the empty booth. No one else was interested in it, so Erika and Henri were able to finally sit down in a seat with a back on it.

Hank came along to take their order, and soon they were elbow deep in ice cream and French fries.

Mike and J.J. had finally decided there would be no news about Mrs. Montague for a while. So they showed up at Deano's, too. When the girls saw them come in, they waved them over.

"Hi, girls. How's the food?" J.J. inquired.

"Delicious. Will you join us?" Henri offered.

There were no other seats in the place, so the boys sat down. They weren't sure they wanted to share what was happening. However, these two girls were their good friends.

"You two don't look very happy. Is there something wrong?" Erika asked.

"Yes," replied Mike. "We stumbled onto a kidnapping right next door to J.J.'s house. Two robbers kidnapped J.J.'s neighbor, Mrs. Montague, at gunpoint. They tied her hands and pushed her into the backseat of a car and drove off. We called 9-1-1, but the police got there after the kidnappers left. No one knows where they are."

"Why didn't you try to follow them?" Henri wondered out loud. "That's what I would have done."

"I don't know," J.J. replied. "I think we were in shock. That never occurred to us. Maybe we weren't thinking well because they had a gun, and the dispatcher told us to stay inside."

"Too late now," Erika added. "What are the police doing?"

"They found the kidnappers' car," Mike continued. "It had been stolen from a city north of here. They must have had another vehicle waiting so the police wouldn't recognize it while they made their escape. The police said just to wait and see if they call asking for a ransom. They will work out a plan after they hear from the kidnappers."

"I feel so helpless," J.J. said. "We don't know where to look or what to do."

"Poor Mrs. Montague. She must have been badly frightened," commented Henri.

"I'm sure she was," said Mike. "I hope she doesn't have a heart attack."

"Why don't you guys order something and try to relax?" Henri suggested. "I know this is hard on you, but there's nothing you can do right now. We'll keep you company."

"Okay," J.J. answered. "I am kind of hungry. That's why we came here. Furthermore, we needed to get out of the house." They ordered fries and Cokes.

It didn't take long for the boys to start talking about sports. They slowed down a little when their food came. This let the girls get in some questions. "What are you two doing for the rest of the summer?" Henri asked. "Are you going anywhere?"

"No trips planned," both boys answered. "There are a couple of books I want to read," added J.J. "I was also considering an online pre-algebra workshop next month. I thought it would make the regular class in September a little easier. The cost is only $15 for four sessions."

"I like that idea," Erika responded. "Why don't we take it together? Then we can discuss what we learn and help each other understand it better."

"Okay. Let's meet at the library tomorrow and use their computer to register. The library opens at eleven o'clock. I'll meet you there."

"I'll be there," Erika said.

"Would you three like to schedule another swimming party?" Henri inquired. "Erika and I plan to go out to Gramma Tessie's house at least once every week of summer vacation. You guys can come along whenever you want to."

"That would be great," Mike added. "Could we ride our bikes out there sometime?"

"Yes, Mike, we could. Erika and I have already talked about doing that. It would be more fun if there were four of us. Maybe Gramma Tessie will let us come on the same day every week."

"I almost forgot," Erika spoke again. "I just met a cool girl and her brother who are staying with their grandmother at Heart Lake. I told her we would call her tomorrow after I talked to you about her, Henri. She seemed really neat and quite lonely."

"Sure. Call her and get her address. We can look her up the next time we're at the lake."

After they finished their food, the boys said they needed to get back to J.J.'s. "I want to be there if the kidnappers call," Mike said.

"Me, too," added J.J. "Call one of us when you decide on a swimming day. We'll try to make it. I'll have to get the flat tire on my bike repaired before I can ride anywhere. I'll do that tomorrow," J.J. stated. "Come on, Mike. Let's get back to my place."

The two girls smiled at the boys as they were leaving. "This should be fun," Erika added. "I think you will like Ann and her brother. I wonder if they like to play board games. I hope they are not hooked on video games. I'm so not into that."

"Me neither. Erika, what do you think about the kidnapping? It sounded scary."

"I thought so, too."

"I'm glad the boys didn't try to follow the kidnappers. Guns are serious business. My dad used to have a gun. He took me shooting at the indoor range a couple of times. He said I needed to know how to use and respect a firearm. The shooting range was very loud, but we wore ear protection. I liked shooting the handguns. I think Mom got rid of the gun after Dad disappeared. I think I'll ask her about it."

"I've never shot a gun. What does your mom think about guns?"

Henri thought for a minute before answering. "She doesn't like guns. She thought it was very dangerous to have a gun in the house. Mom didn't think girls should have anything to do with guns. Dad took me to two gun safety workshops the year before he disappeared. I learned a lot."

"I'm done with my banana split. The walk home will do me good. I feel like I just gained four pounds. Let's go. It's beginning to get noisy in here."

"It's getting crowded, too. Let's go," Henri agreed.

"Okay. My little brother is staying with our grandparents for this entire next week. I'm sure I won't miss him at all."

"Well, don't say that to him. You need to keep your brother as your friend."

Erika answered that comment very quickly. "We get along very well. He's okay for a younger brother. He likes to spend much of his time in his room. But he's always doing things for me. If I misplace something, he usually finds it."

"Let's give J.J. a call in the morning to see if the police have any leads on the kidnappers."

"Okay. Come over around 9:30 tomorrow morning, and we'll call from my house. Now, I think I'm ready for a little walk to work off this ice cream. I should have ordered a regular size banana split instead of a large."

The two girls got up and walked to the cash register. They each had to pay their bill. Soon they were walking west towards Monroe Street. That was where Henri went north and Erika went south.

11

THE ROBBERS HAD PANICKED. WHEN THEY FOUND NOTHING valuable to steal, they decided to take Mrs. Montague with them. Perhaps the neighbors would pay a ransom to get her back. They had watched the house for a couple of weeks and had seen her neighbors visit her several times.

"Slow down, Jeb!" Boyd shouted. "You'll attract attention. We don't want to get pulled over by a cop."

"Okay, okay. I'll try to, but we've just kidnapped an old woman. Now, we have to figure out what to do with her."

"First, we switch cars at the warehouse. Then we need to find a place to hide out for a while."

"Please let me out. I won't press charges if you just let me go. I have no family and I'm not rich. You have nothing to gain by keeping me," pleaded Mrs. Montague.

"Shut up!" yelled Boyd. "If you speak again, I'll duct tape your mouth."

"You wouldn't dare! Don't you touch me!"

Boyd pulled off a piece of duct tape from the roll on the floor and used his teeth to cut it. He grabbed her hair and pulled her head back. Angrily, he slapped the tape over her mouth. "That'll keep you quiet."

"Will you settle down?" Jeb sternly reprimanded his partner. "Things will be okay. I remember seeing an old cabin a couple of miles from the main road in heavy timber over by Heart Lake. We hiked in there many years ago. It was hard going. I don't think anyone uses it. What do you think about going there?"

"We can go and see. There's a store on the way there. We can get some supplies in case we have to stay there a while. My house is on the way, so we can get some pillows and blankets."

Jeb headed north after they switched cars. No one had been around the warehouse, so they were quite sure their car was unknown to the police. Boyd pushed Mrs. Montague down onto the seat and held her there as they drove so no one could see her. They did not want her to see Boyd's house either.

They picked up some blankets and pillows, some extra clothes, and finally provisions from the small store near Heart Lake. Jeb found a trail off the dirt road and pulled the car in and around a bend. It could not be seen if anyone came along the road.

"I figure it's a short hike to the cabin from here. We can take the old woman over and tie her to a chair. Then we can come back for everything else."

"Good idea. Help me get her out of the car." Jeb was a lot nicer to Mrs. Montague. "Don't worry, ma'am, we're not going to hurt you. We will contact your neighbors and offer you back for a few thousand dollars. You'll be free in no time."

A short walk brought them to a cabin in dense brush and trees. The area had not been cleared in a long time. The cabin blended in very well. There was a second cabin near it, but that looked abandoned, too.

Both men were surprised to see two chairs on the front porch and a blanket hanging from an improvised clothesline. "It looks like someone might be living here," Jeb said. He took out his gun as they approached the place. He kicked the door open and poked the gun inside. "Put your hands up and no one gets hurt," he ordered.

The cabin was empty. However, there were dishes in the sink and some sleeping bags and blankets piled in the corner. "Someone is staying here, that's for sure," Boyd observed. "What should we do?"

"Maybe they won't be back. If they do return, I'll shoot them. We need this place to stay in for a few days before we head up into Canada like we planned."

They tied Mrs. Montague to a chair and were about to go back to the car when they heard someone step onto the wooden porch. Jeb pulled his gun from his waistband again and aimed it at the door.

Zolar walked in. He was in his alien form and screamed at the intruders as he made a rush at them. Jeb shot him three times in the chest. As the bullets tore into him, Zolar was thrown back into the door that had closed behind him. He was dead before he hit the floor. His body turned a bright golden orange color and then totally disintegrated into nothing.

"What was that thing?" Boyd muttered in a daze.

"I don't know. It looked human, except for the long head and big ears. That glowing gold skin scared me. Do you think there are more of them?"

"We better look around outside and see. I don't want to be taken by surprise."

Dagnaut and Joblanc were quite a ways behind Zolar. He had gone ahead to get dinner started. Both aliens shuddered when they heard the gunshots.

They took out their weapons and slowly made their way toward the cabin. Dagnaut went off to the right while Joblanc stayed facing the front. They remained in the dense bushes about twenty feet from the front door. They saw two men exit the cabin and stand on the porch, screaming.

"Are there any more of you golden zombies out there? Show yourselves! We're gonna shoot you just like we did the one inside the cabin. Then you can dissolve into nothing, and we'll be done with you." Jeb and Boyd came down the steps of the cabin right in front of Joblanc. Jeb shot into a nearby tree for emphasis. "Come on out, you creeps!"

At this point, Dagnaut nodded to Joblanc and raised his weapon. He pointed at Joblanc and then to the right.

He pointed at himself and then to the left. They both fired at the same time. There was a sort of snorting sound that came from each of their weapons. A brilliant white light flashed and shot out towards Boyd and Jeb. They were both hit in the chest and crumpled to the ground, each quite dead from the electrical laser type bolt they had been struck with.

"You heard the shots," Joblanc said with much concern in his voice. "Do you think he killed Zolar?"

"Yes. Did you hear him call us golden zombies? Zolar must have transformed back to his native state before he entered the cabin. How else would the humans know that we dissolve into nothing when we die on Earth?"

"What will we do without Zolar?"

"We will be fine. We must notify the base. We need to return to Saros soon. Perhaps Colonel Jabu will send a replacement back with us. We should go inside and see what they did to our cabin."

They approached the door of the cabin very slowly. They heard nothing from inside as they crept up the steps, weapons at the ready. They saw Mrs. Montague tied to the chair. She was facing away from them.

"What do we do with her?" Joblanc asked. "I do not want to shoot a woman."

"I think she was kidnapped. We should figure out how to release her without letting her see us."

"Good idea. I will put a towel over her head and tell her what we intend to do. I hope that helps keep her calm."

"Miss," Joblanc spoke as he carefully covered her head and face with a towel. "We are here to rescue you. We have taken care of the two men who tied you up. Just relax and we will take you someplace where you will be found." He removed the duct tape slowly from her mouth. "Please do not scream."

"Why are you covering my face if you are rescuing me?" she asked.

"We do not want you to see us. We are not connected to the men who took you. We do not know who they are. Please try to remain calm. We will untie your feet and walk you out of the woods. Then we will drop you off next to a small market. Do you understand?"

"Yes, I do. Thank you."

The two men untied her feet and walked her out a different direction to their car. They put her inside and drove to a small convenience market on the edge of Hartford. "Please do not yell for help yet. Let us drive off first," Dagnaut requested.

"Okay," she replied. "Thanks again."

They took her out of the car and sat her down on the side of the store where there were no cameras.

"I must ask you again to let us drive away before you holler for someone inside the store to come out and help you. We will not remove the towel from your eyes. You will be okay. Count to one hundred slowly and then yell for help, okay?"

"I'll do just as you ask."

Joblanc and Dagnaut got into their car and backed out the way they had pulled in next to the market. They were unseen and out of sight when Mrs. Montague began yelling for help.

It only took a few minutes for someone inside the store to hear her yelling. One of the employees came out to see what the noise was and found her sitting up against the wall of the store.

He removed the towel from her head and said, "Who are you? Who did this to you? Are you all right?"

"Slow down, sonny," she replied. "I'm all right. Just a little shaken I believe, but I'm very happy to be alive. My name is Alice Montague. Two men kidnapped me a couple of hours ago in Millville. They drove me to a cabin someplace around here. They were holding me for ransom. Three other men came along, and I think they killed my kidnappers in a gunfight. I am quite sure one of the rescuers was also killed. They told me they did not want me to see their faces but that they would set me free. They drove me here just a few minutes ago. I think you should call 9-1-1!"

"First, let me untie you and get you inside the store. I'll get you something to drink." When he got her inside, he shouted to the other employee, "Call 9-1-1! This is an emergency! What is your name again, ma'am?" he asked turning back to the woman.

"Mrs. Alice Montague," she replied with a warm smile. She was happy to be safe and free from those terrible men.

"Tell the police where we are located and that we have found Mrs. Alice Montague who was kidnapped from Millville."

Four squad cars arrived from Millville a few minutes later. Shortly after that two police cars arrived from Hartford. The officers all had more questions than Mrs. Montague had answers.

She didn't know the location of the cabin where she had been held. She didn't know the men who had kidnapped her. She was quite sure they were dead. She didn't know or see the men who had rescued her. She wondered why they had covered her eyes.

Finally, she said, "Will you please take me home? My neighbors are probably really worried about me."

"Yes, we can take you home right now," officer Cole told her. We'd like you to come by the station tomorrow and look at some photos. You might be able to pick out the men who kidnapped you."

"I'll do that. Right now, I just want to go home," Mrs. Montague replied with a long sigh.

The police had a few questions for the store employee who found Mrs. Montague. He had neither seen nor heard the men who dropped her off beside the store. The security camera had no pictures from the area where she had been found.

It was nearly 8:30 when the squad car pulled into Mrs. Montague's driveway. The station had called Mrs. Jamison to tell her Mrs. Montague had been found and that she was safe and on her way home.

Mrs. Jamison, J.J., Mike, and Jerry were all sitting on their front porch when the police car pulled in next door. They all ran to greet and hug Mrs. Montague.

"It's so good to see friends again," Mrs. Montague sobbed. Her eyes were filled with tears as Mrs. Jamison held her tight. "You folks are such good neighbors. I thought I might never see you again."

"We never gave up hope," Mrs. Jamison reassured her while wiping away her own tears with one hand and still hugging Mrs. Montague with the other one. "We knew you would come home safely. Let's get you inside and sit down for a while."

The police searched the house and then left with a promise to post a guard outside all night.

When they were all seated in her small living room, Mrs. Montague started to tell the story about her kidnapping. She kept them spellbound as she related all the events that had happened to her. The gunfire had really scared her, although she didn't see any of it.

"I'm glad to be safe at home again. I hope nothing like that ever happens to me again. I could have a heart attack from all this excitement," she laughed. She had quite a sense of humor, and the Jamisons considered her part of their family.

"Do you want one of us to stay with you tonight?" J.J. asked.

"No, I won't need that with a policeman outside all night. I don't think I'll be afraid with those evil men being dead. I'll be safe enough."

After walking across Mrs. Montague's yard and crossing his driveway, the thought of calling Henri came to J.J. He hurried inside to make the call.

"Hello," answered Mrs. Matthews after the fifth ring.

"Hi, Mrs. Matthews. It's J.J. Is Henri there?"

"Sure, I'll get her. Sorry it took so long to answer. We were sitting on the front porch. Is there any news about Mrs. Montague?"

"Yes. The police found her, and she is safely back home."

"That's great news. Here's Henri."

"Hi, J.J. What's great news?" Henri asked.

"Mrs. Montague has been rescued and is safely home. She's okay, and the police have posted an all-night guard at her house."

"That's fantastic! I know how much you were worried about her. Do you know how she was rescued?"

"Mrs. Montague said the kidnappers tried to hide out in a cabin somewhere. When the three residents returned, there was a gunfight. The two kidnappers apparently were killed as was one of the cabin residents. Mrs. Montague came through the ordeal unhurt. She has a lot of spunk for an eighty-five-year-old lady."

"I'm so glad she's safe. I hate to hear about anyone being killed, but at least she won't have to worry about them coming after her again. Does she know why they kidnapped her?"

"She said the robbers were a bit confused and disorganized. She thought they just wanted to rob her but found nothing to steal. So they decided to kidnap her and see if we would pay a ransom to get her back. She heard them talking and arguing about what to do and where to hide out. She heard them say they were heading to Canada after getting some hostage money."

"Were the robbers local guys?"

"The police didn't say. I'm glad it's over for Mrs. Montague. Why don't you stop over tomorrow morning and we'll go see her?"

"Okay. Can I bring Erika along?"

"Sure. That'll be fine. Come over around ten o'clock, okay?"

"See you then. Bye."

"Bye, Henri."

. . . .

Dagnaut and Joblanc were going to miss Zolar. There was nothing they could do but continue with the surveillance. They went back to the cabin, and after putting on gloves, they wrapped the men in two blankets. They did some searching around their cabin and found the car the robbers had used. Joblanc drove the robbers' car and Dagnaut drove their car to the far side of Hartford, looking for a place to dispose of the evidence.

There were four lakes nearby and several hundred cabins. They finally found a single cabin that looked deserted at the end of a gravel road. They knocked on the door, ready to pretend they were lost if anyone answered. When no one did, they picked the lock and went inside. They made it look like someone had been staying there. Some food was left around and the two beds were pulled open to look like someone had slept in them.

Joblanc parked the kidnappers' car in the driveway, and they carried the two men from the trunk and placed them on the porch to make it look like they had fallen there after being shot. They left the cabin door open when they left. They removed their gloves as they slowly drove away.

Several days later, the Hartford police got a call from a hiker near Grass Lake. He reported seeing two bodies on the porch of a cabin in a secluded area.

The police sent two units out to investigate. They found two men who had been dead several days lying on the porch of a small cabin. After further investigation, they were suspected of being the kidnappers. Mrs. Montague and Mrs. Jamison had to go to the police station to look at pictures of the men. Mrs. Montague identified them as her abductors.

The medical examiner concluded in his report that the men had died of heart failure. There were small burn marks on the chest of each man. He could not determine what caused them. The time of their deaths coincided with the day Mrs. Montague had been rescued.

The police thought it unusual that both men would have similar burns on their chests and die from heart failure at the same time. They found no other clues, and after several months, the case was closed.

12

Dr. Emory's first two days on Saros had been spent at the secret government base he reported to. Forty-eight hours of cellular regeneration had made him feel rejuvenated.

"I feel ten years younger, Commander," he remarked upon awakening from a two-day sleep.

"You look great," Commander Tammer replied. "Are you ready to get to work?"

"I sure am. My first thing to do is visit the underground caves of the mystics. My lab is there, and I have an idea to check out. Next will be your briefing regarding the situation here on Saros. I'll be back to meet you in four days. We can make plans then."

"That will be fine. The underground military has made threats, so I am sending armed soldiers with you. We will meet here for breakfast four days from right now."

Transportation was waiting to take Dr. M to the Millennial Chapel building in the center of the city. From there, he would secretly be taken by underground rail five miles south outside the city. Two soldiers accompanied him. Armed military transport would meet him there and take him further into the rugged terrain of Saros. Once there, he would enter the Cave of the Alugets. This was where he would meet the Elders of Saros and start work at his secret workshop.

When they arrived at the chapel, they took the elevator down to the railway station. There was a railcar waiting for them, and the two soldiers boarded with Dr. M. It took only ten minutes to reach the next station outside the city. The railcar came to a stop at the small underground switching station.

Dr. M was a little nervous. The threats by the underground military must be taken seriously. *They wouldn't dare attack this close to the city, would they?* he thought.

They exited the railcar and entered the station room. There were five guards stationed around the room, alertly watching their arrival. As Dr. M and his two escorts entered, the five soldiers suddenly raised their weapons.

"Do not move," one of the soldiers said. "Place your weapons on the floor."

"Do as he says," Dr. M stated. "There's nothing else you can do."

A highly decorated officer stepped from behind a barricade. "That is a wise decision. There is no need for anyone to get hurt." Then he said to one of his soldiers, "Collect their weapons. When the elevator returns, follow us to the surface and confine these two men in the kitchen."

He turned back and spoke in a friendly but serious voice, "Greetings, Dr. M. It is a pleasure to finally meet you. I am Colonel Jabu." The man was tall, slender, and had a strict military bearing. His weathered face and serious countenance showed experience and determination. "You will not be harmed. I only want to talk with you and exchange ideas. Please enter the elevator, and we will discuss matters in a more relaxed atmosphere."

Dr. M remained silent. They entered the elevator and rose to the surface. Two of Colonel Jabu's soldiers accompanied them. The door opened to a large room with windows on two sides. He could see several more buildings outside. There were military people moving around. *This looks like a military base. I did not come this way the last time I visited the mystics,* he thought.

Finally, he spoke, "How did you get in here? This is a government military base."

"Oh, we have our ways. When the future of an entire planet hangs in the balance, many obstacles can be overcome. We have many supporters in the government and your military who think our plan is the best one."

"What do you want?"

"To start with, I want to explain our position to you. I do not think the current government understands the feelings of the majority of the people of Saros. We will talk about that first and see where it leads."

"Am I a prisoner?"

"Let us say you are being detained for a short time. We will determine your status after we talk."

"Okay. Let's talk," Dr. M replied, trying to maintain a positive and friendly attitude. *There's no sense making him mad,* he thought. *My best hope is to play along and see what I can learn. There is no escape at present.*

"You have made another wise decision. I see why the government holds you in such high regard. We will talk in a more comfortable room. Colonel Jabu walked toward one of the doors that a soldier promptly opened.

"After you," he offered.

"Thank you."

They walked down a long hallway that led to a door that opened into a large room. Here, food and drinks had been prepared. Four more soldiers sat around tables eating and talking quietly. They jumped to their feet and saluted as Colonel Jabu entered the room.

He returned the salutes and stated, "As you were."

They sat at a table apart from the others. Drinks were brought to the table, and the colonel proposed a toast. He raised his glass and said, "To cooperation and understanding. May the future of Saros be peaceful and prosperous."

"I can drink to that," Dr. M added.

"See, we both want peace. However, we have to save our planet."

"I agree, but not at the expense of Earth."

"Do you know that nearly half the people of Saros favor attacking Earth and taking its water? We have ten thousand people who want to go to Earth to live. If we could solve the problem of the yellow sun disease, we could send them to Earth right now. Earth would welcome our technology."

"That's where you are wrong, Colonel Jabu. I have been working on Earth for many years, and they will not cooperate. Even if faced with an interplanetary war, they will not share their water or their planet. I will continue to talk with their leaders and try to convince them of the benefits of cooperation. In time, they might come around."

Raising his voice, Colonel Jabu responded, "Then they will suffer the consequences. We do not have time! We are preparing for an invasion within a year! Tell me what you have discovered regarding the magno-pulse machine you have been working on."

"I am afraid there's nothing new to report. I think the machine is a failure," he lied. "I have not been able to make any improvements. My experience is leading me to the conclusion that something in my genes is making me immune to the yellow sun's radiation. The longer I am there, the stronger I get. Our doctors have examined me but could find nothing out of the ordinary to explain my growing immunity. The good part of that is I will have more time to work on Earth to convince them to cooperate with us for their own benefit."

"You are lying! You have been using your machine, and that is how you have been able to safely stay there several months. Is that right?"

"Yes, but I am concluding that it is not the machine that is keeping me alive."

"If that is the truth, then give us your machine and we will test it on some of our people and see if your conclusion is valid."

"And if it is not, then your people will get very sick and perhaps die."

"They are willing to take that chance. We can always bring them back to Saros in time to save them."

"My machine is in my laboratory. I will have to think about your proposal. It would be good to test my hypothesis. However, if the machine did work for your people, then it would strengthen your invasion plans. That is not a good idea."

"You have no choice."

Just then there was a commotion outside. Three ships that looked like flying cabin cruisers landed in the open space about twenty-five yards away. The men inside the building heard loud bursts of buzzing as soldiers jumped out of the ships. Everyone outside collapsed under the soldiers' fire.

Colonel Jabu's soldiers raised their weapons and rushed to the windows to see what was happening.

"Government reinforcements have arrived. They are paralyzing everyone," Colonel Jabu stated in a matter-of-fact tone.

The loyal underground troops looked to him for direction. "What should we do? Do we shoot back?" one of them asked.

"No. We came here to talk with Dr. M. It seems we have been discovered. Dr. M, we mean you no harm. You must understand that many of our people want Earth's water. We will make a deal for it, or they will support a war to take it. If you cannot get the government to cooperate with us, then there will be a revolt. Your government will be overthrown. You will be on the wrong side of the conflict. You must talk to Commander Tammer. Tell him what I have said. You will hear from me again. Next time, I might not be so cooperative."

With that Colonel Jabu and his soldiers rushed through the doorway down the long hallway back to the room where the elevator was. They went down to the lower level where the solitary railcar sat waiting. There were no guards, so they climbed aboard and made their escape.

Seven heavily armed government troops rushed into the room. The lieutenant in charge recognized Dr. M and addressed him. "Is everyone in here okay?"

"Yes," responded Dr. M, "but Colonel Jabu got away. He and his soldiers went through that door back to the elevator to the rail system below."

"Check that out," Lieutenant Jacobs ordered. Six soldiers slowly went down the hallway to the elevator. When they got to the subterranean rail system, the railcar was gone. There was no way to give chase.

"They are gone," a soldier reported back to Lieutenant Jacobs.

One of the servers came up to them and said in a meek voice, "Excuse me, Sir. There are some soldiers tied up in the kitchen. They were captured when the other soldiers arrived a couple of hours ago."

"Thank you. Sergeant Hadley, take your men and free those soldiers."

"Yes, sir," he replied.

"What happened here?" Lieutenant Jacobs asked Dr. M.

"Colonel Jabu wanted to talk to me. He left rather quickly when you arrived."

"What did he want?"

"He gave me a message for Commander Tammer. We are scheduled to meet in four days. The message can wait until then. You had better check the security on the railway. Somehow Colonel Jabu was able to gain access and nearly kidnap me."

"I will get on it right away. Six of my men will escort you on the rest of your trip. Follow them and they will take you to the other station across the base."

"Thank you."

Dr. M was escorted across the base to a much larger subterranean rail station. Soon he was again on his way but with a much larger escort.

13

AFTER THE INTERESTING MEETING WITH COLONEL JABU, DR. M finally arrived at the caves of the mystics. Lebu, head of the Elders, warmly greeted him.

"Welcome, Dr. M. We have been expecting you. Everything is prepared as you requested in your communication while en route to Saros."

"Thank you, Lebu. Did you secure the special Saros stones for me?"

"Yes. Be very careful with them. They are the last of their kind. Everything will depend on how they are used."

"I am aware of the seriousness of my mission. Would you take me to the Room of Sacred Wisdom, please? I need to consult the prophecies. Grams and Tess have identified three of the four 'Promised Ones.' They believe the fourth has also been located, but I need confirmation."

"Follow me."

They went much deeper into the caverns. There were many turns with several side tunnels. Dr. M was quite sure he would not be able to find his way out without Lebu's guidance.

"Here we are. You must purify yourself before entering."

After going through the purification ritual, Dr. M entered a dimly lit cavern. He could not see the ceiling, as the light did not illuminate that far up. Slowly, he approached the glowing wall in front of him. As he placed his hands flat against it, a strange but not surprising thing happened to him. He was drawn into the wall. It seemed to absorb him. He felt like he was floating in space but was completely relaxed. This was his third visit here.

A bright glowing ball materialized in front of him. A voice emanated from within it and said, "State your request."

"I wish to view the prophecy."

Then words began to appear within the ball. A voice spoke the compelling words of the prophecy:

"FOUR WILL BE BORN FAR AWAY. A YELLOW SUN MARKS THEIR ORIGIN. A PLANET, MOSTLY WATER, WITH ONE MOON WILL BE THEIR HOME. ANCESTORS WILL BE TRACED TO SAROS. TWO TEAMS OF TWO WITH SAROS STONES MERGE TO PROMOTE SPECIAL POWERS AND ABILITIES.

YOUNG WILL THEY BE WHEN THEIR TRAINING BEGINS. ALL HOPE IS WITH THEM. BUT BEWARE...A DANGER...ONE POWERFUL BUT EVIL EMERGES FOR A TIME..."

The glow faded and Dr. M was pushed back through the translucent wall. He was standing just as he had entered with his hands flat against it.

Lebu was waiting at the cavern entrance. "Did you find what you came for?"

"Yes. All is not clear, but I know enough to proceed. Thank you for your assistance. Please take me to my lab now."

"As you wish." Lebu led the way through the dimly lit maze of tunnels. They were about halfway back when he made a turn into a dark corridor. He switched on his light pack and reached to the ceiling. He pressed two stones that looked like all the others, and the entire wall ahead of them slid silently away.

They passed through the opening and entered a very large cavern. It had adequate lighting and contained a fully equipped science research laboratory. Two Saronians sat working in front of two computers.

"Welcome home," they greeted. "All is prepared as you requested. No one has entered your personal lab."

"Greetings, Sal and Jub. Thank you for making preparations for me. Continue your work." *I'm not surprised no one has entered my lab,* he thought. *Lebu and I are the only ones who know the stone sequence to cross the chasm.*

"How long will you require?" Lebu asked.

"Three days."

"Then I will return in three days."

"Thank you."

Lebu left the lab.

"Here are the machine components you asked us to make," Sal said. "We finished them yesterday."

"Thank you. I will take them with me into my lab. Please put them into a bag."

"Certainly," replied Sal. Jub brought a bag over, and they put the electronic pieces they had made into it. Sal handed it to Dr. M.

"Thank you. That will be all," Dr. M said. He walked over to one of the rough rock walls of the cavern. He put his face up to a small aperture. A light flashed and a click sounded. Slowly, a rock in the wall moved aside, revealing a keypad. Dr. M pressed a series of twelve numbers. As he removed his hand, the rock slid back into place.

Then the wall in front of him slid away, and he took three steps forward. The opening closed behind him. Automatic lights came on to reveal the four-foot square ledge he was standing on. In front of him was a five-foot wide path leading across a span of fifteen feet. It was covered with flat stones, each about twenty inches wide. There was a Saronian symbol on each one. A faulty step would plunge an intruder over one hundred feet to the rocky cavern floor below.

"Maintain your balance. Watch your step. You know the sequence," he said out loud. Carefully, he stepped on the proper stones and safely crossed the dangerous path.

Once across, he placed his hands on two different stones in the wall ahead of him. The wall slid away creating a doorway. He stepped into his private lab, and the wall closed behind him. Lights came on to reveal a room approximately twenty feet by fifteen feet.

There was a workbench and a stool on one wall and several pieces of specialized equipment on two tables. One wall had a large computer screen in front of a computer keyboard. Dr. M walked across the room, placed the components on the bench, and sat in the chair in front of the computer station.

It took three days of work before he electronically recorded his findings. "I have successfully altered the genetic structure of my DNA by using the new enhanced magno-pulse machine. It now must be tested on Earth. My calculations show my cellular structure to be compatible with Earth's yellow sun. There will be no cellular degeneration. This is the breakthrough I had hoped for."

Dr. M packed one of the two new, smaller magno-pulse machines in a briefcase-size leather satchel. Then he set the combination lock, as well as the acid release valve, in case someone tried to break into the satchel. Next, he carefully put the second magno-pulse machine into a hidden wall safe. It was also inside an acid protected satchel. He closed the door to the safe and pushed a button on the wall next to it. The door to the safe and the button became invisible.

He went to his replicator. After pressing a few keys, a duplicate of the magno-pulse was made. He removed the critical parts and replaced them with others that Sal and Jub had made earlier. These parts were nonworking and would lead anyone trying to discover their secret in the wrong direction.

This fake magno-pulse machine was then placed inside a satchel nearly like the original satchel he was taking to Earth. It also had an acid protection system, but this one would not harm the components when forced open.

Next, he took the extra original parts and put them into a small metal heating unit. They were heated until they melted. He tilted the machine and poured them into a square mold. When they hardened, no one would know what they had been.

Finally, he turned off the power to his lab. His work here was completed. He was ready to return to the city.

"That's all for now," he told Sal and Jub as he came out into the main lab. He set the security system to seal his personal lab. "Let's go back to the surface."

Lebu was waiting in the tunnel outside the big cavern. He guided them back through the maze of tunnels to the surface. Dr. M was glad to be outside again, although seeing the dull red sun felt a little strange after living under the brilliant yellow sun of Earth.

There was a twenty-man military escort waiting for him. Commander Tammer himself was leading it. "We captured one of the militants. He works for Captain Stamtu of the underground military. He said they had talked about kidnapping you to get the magno-pulse. We will provide you with a larger escort from now on."

"Thank you. I will feel much safer with a larger escort."

"Where to next?" Commander Tammer inquired.

"Back to government headquarters. I have accomplished everything scheduled for now. Let's go back and talk about what to do to prevent a war."

They returned to the central headquarters just as night was falling. There were sleeping quarters inside the complex. The military and government employees never had to leave the security of the complex. It comprised three square miles and had heavy security in and around it.

The two men met for breakfast early the next morning. Commander Tammer started the discussion. "The man we captured said that the underground military has been heavily recruiting. He says they will now be known as the Progressive Save Saros Government or the PSSG. They want to have elections and take over the government. Their premise is that they can provide water and save Saros."

"Did he tell you how they plan to get the water?" Dr. M asked.

"Yes. If Earth does not voluntarily offer some of its water in exchange for technology, then Saros will invade

Earth. Saronians will become permanent residents there, and water will be sent back to Saros."

"Colonel Jabu told me the same thing. He said there was growing support for their position. I tend to agree with him on that score. Can you maintain control of the government?"

"Yes, for a while. The more critical the water shortage gets, the more support the PSSG will garner. It is conceivable they could force a vote by the people. The PSSG could win control of the government. Even if we win an election, we could have a revolt on our hands if we do not give in to their demands."

After talking for nearly two hours, Dr. M was ready to rest. Preparations were being made for his return to Earth for the day after tomorrow. He had the Saros stones, the enhanced magno-pulse, and a better understanding of the underground military's plans. He was ready to return to Earth.

14

GRAMS GOT UP WHEN TESS DROVE IN AND WENT TO A SECRET control room inside her house. It was a cleverly built room off one of the interior walls. The small control room had been built behind a closet and underneath the wide stairway that led to the second level of the farmhouse. There was a shoe storage rack that blocked the concealed door in the back of the closet. A hidden button would cause it to swing away from the wall. Another button hidden on the back of the shoe rack would open the door to the small room.

Grams entered the room. It had communications equipment plus two TV screens. These were connected to the satellite dishes mounted on the roof. The dishes were in a recessed area so they could not be seen from the ground.

She activated the screens that brought her constant news from all over the world. Grams also turned on the jamming system that sent out undetectable gamma neutrons. These invisible electronic rays made it impossible for anything being said in the house to be heard or recorded.

She walked back to the living room and sat down to wait.

Knock, knock, knock.

"Come in, Tess. I'm in the front room."

Tess entered and met Grams face to face. "Is this an emergency? What have you learned?" she asked in an alarmed tone.

"First, let's lock the door you came in through. Then we will go into the control room." She double locked the door, and they went into the small room. There were five chairs in this room, and they sat down to talk. Grams pushed a button on the keyboard on the desk. The door closed, and the bookcase slid back into place.

"Now, we can talk. Dr. M sent me a transmission from Saros. The military is getting ready to invade Earth about a year from now. Three men have already landed here. Another ship with thirteen Saronians aboard will be arriving here in six months."

"What should we do?"

"We are to talk with J.J. and Henri. They need to know about each other. It will help them to be more comfortable with their new powers if they know they are not alone. Dr. M will start working with them when he returns. They already trust him, so knowing about him will help them adjust."

"Do we tell them we are aliens? How do we explain knowing about their powers? Will they trust us?"

"I already spoke with J.J. He was a bit overwhelmed. He had trouble understanding that I knew about the power of his Saros stone. He also wondered how I knew about the lives he had just saved."

"Did he ask you how you knew?"

"Yes. I talked around it a little. I told him he would learn more in the next few weeks. He is expecting to discover another person who has a power similar to his. He needs someone to talk to and relate what he's feeling."

"So we need to get the two of them together?"

"Yes, as soon as possible. I think we should invite them out for a pizza lunch at your place. Just the two of them. Let's have them arrive together and ask them to tell no one but their parents where they are going. Say it is extremely important that you talk with the two of them. Then say you must take them someplace else for this talk. Drive them over here, but do not take a direct route. We do not want you to be followed."

"I can do that," Tess said, accepting her role in this new development. "Should I call them when I get home?"

"Yes," replied Grams. "But be very vague in what you say. If the aliens have discovered Dr. M is here, they might be watching us also. We do not know if they can tell if we are from Saros, so we must not take any chances."

"I'll be careful. I'll call to tell you a day and time when we can all get together. I will use a code to give you the details. I'll say, nice weather we are having. Right after weather, a letter and a time will be inserted. *A-twelve o'clock* will mean Sunday at ten o'clock. *B-two o'clock* will be Monday at twelve o'clock. *C-three o'clock* will be Tuesday at one o'clock. Subtract two hours from the time I suggest. Will that work?"

"That'll be fine. If someone is listening on your phones, this will throw them off."

Tess had another idea. "I think I'll go into town and make my calls from the library telephone. The librarian is a good friend, and she will let me use her office to make the calls."

"What a great idea! Call me when the meeting is set."

"Okay. What else will we need to tell them?"

"I think we should tell them about each other's power. Then we'll let them talk privately for a few minutes. We can return and try to answer any questions they have. Let's not mention Dr. M or Saros right now."

"That's good. We should give them some proof about who we are, though. They should be able to handle seeing us as aliens. First, we can tell them how we came here and that they really are related to us. Then let's see how they react."

"Okay. Dr. M said we should tell them as much as we feel necessary. They need to be prepared for their roles to help save Earth, as well as Saros, when the time arrives."

Tess had still another concern. "Do you think they will be bothered about being part Saronian? We need to be prepared to explain that to them."

"We need to be ready to tell them the entire story of how we came here. I think we should let Dr. M handle the part about the prophecies," Grams concluded.

"I agree. I'll go and make those calls now." She got up as Grams pushed the button to open the door. Grams also turned off the jammer and news screens. They would not need those at present.

Once outside the secret room, Grams closed the door and the shoe rack returned to its normal place. As they walked to the door to the outside, Tess wistfully said, "This is all like a dream. We knew this day would come. I always hoped things would work out peacefully without a big conflict."

"Who knows?" Grams countered. "We may find a peaceful solution. If these are the 'Promised Ones', their powers may save both planets and possibly even without a war."

"Let's hope that's the way it happens. Goodbye, Grams."

"Good-bye, Tess." They hugged and Tess drove away toward town.

Grams sat on the porch a long time after Tess left, thinking about what the future would bring. She hoped it would be peace and cooperation between two very different planets.

15

At ten o'clock, Henri and Erika walked up the driveway to J.J.'s house. The boys saw them and came down the porch steps to greet them.

"Hi, J.J. Hi, Mike," both girls sang out. It was a happy new day because Mrs. Montague had been freed.

"Hi, girls," Mike and J.J. replied. "Isn't it a beautiful day?" Mike added.

"It sure is," exclaimed Henri. "Can we go see Mrs. Montague?"

"She's expecting us. Mom spoke with her last night, and she said we could come over at ten o'clock this morning."

They walked next door to Mrs. Montague's house. When she didn't answer after a second knock, J.J. spoke out, "I don't like this. She knew we were coming over at ten o'clock. It's a little after ten. Something must have happened to her."

"Is the door locked?" asked Henri. She reached out to try the knob. She was always the first one to take action.

The knob turned and the door opened a little. "Should we go in?"

"Yes," Mike said. "Let me go first. Mrs. Montague. Hello. Are you here? Are you all right? It's Mike and J.J. Can you hear me?"

There was no answer.

"Let's all go in and see what's happened," suggested Henri.

The four of them slowly entered the house. It was well lighted as all the curtains were pulled back.

Everything looked okay. It did not look like anyone had broken in. Mike kept calling, "Mrs. Montague, hello, anyone here?"

The door to the bedroom was closed. J.J. knocked gently at first. Then he knocked again and spoke loudly. "Mrs. Montague, are you in the bedroom? Are you okay?"

Still no answer. "We're coming in to check on you. It's J.J., Mike, Henri, and Erika. We're worried about you."

J.J. pushed the door open. As the four of them entered the bedroom, time stood still. Henri had touched her necklace to stop time. She was afraid of what they might find and decided to stop things and take a look first herself.

With the other three frozen like statues, Henri looked around the bedroom. The bed was neatly made. She peeked into the bathroom. No sense asking if Mrs. Montague was here. If she was, she couldn't answer.

The bathroom was as neat as a pin and empty. Where was Mrs. Montague? Henri slipped back through the bedroom and looked in the other bedroom, as well as the pantry. Next, she opened the back door to look outside. There was a small single-car garage out back. She decided to have a look there, too.

She was surprised when she looked through the small windows in the garage door. Mrs. Montague's car was not there. "Oh, no! Someone has kidnapped her again and stolen her car!" she said out loud. "I've got to get back and start time again so we can call the police."

Quickly, she walked back into the house and to the bedroom where the others were. She smiled at herself for hurrying. "I guess I didn't need to hurry. Time is standing still. Nothing is happening anywhere. I hope Mrs. Montague is okay."

She placed her two thumbs against both sides of the stone. Time began again.

"She's not here either," a worried Erika blurted out. "What should we do?"

"Henri and I will check out the rest of the house. Erika and Mike, you go see if her car is in the garage," J.J. ordered.

Before Henri could say anything, a car pulled into the driveway and honked the horn. The kids almost jumped out of their shoes.

It was Mrs. Montague. J.J. and Henri raced out the front door to see who was honking. They were greatly relieved when Mrs. Montague got out of her car and spoke to them.

"Hi, kids. I'm sorry I wasn't here right at ten. I wanted to have something special for you. When I started to mix up a batch of cookies at 8:30, I discovered there wasn't enough sugar or canola oil. So I decided to make a quick run to the store. Mrs. McNeil was there, and we sat down in the deli for a couple of minutes. She wanted to know all about my latest adventure. Her son is Lieutenant McNeil. He is head of the police department. I just lost track of time."

"We were scared!" J.J. spoke up. "We thought you had been kidnapped again. We're sorry we went into your house. First, we thought you might have had a heart attack or something. Sorry, I'm babbling."

"It's okay, J.J. I understand. I'm so thankful to have such concerned neighbors as you and your friends. Come in and we'll eat some of the cookies I bought. When I saw how late it was, I just picked up a couple dozen chocolate chip cookies as well as the baking items I needed."

They all went inside and talked and ate cookies. Mrs. Montague wanted to know what the kids had been doing since school had let out. The kids wanted to know all about her kidnapping experience. They spent a delightful hour exchanging information.

When they got back to J.J.'s porch, Erika spoke up first. "Weren't you guys afraid for Mrs. Montague? My first thought was that she had died from a heart attack and that we would find her lying on the floor or in bed. What a dreadful thought that was. I almost cried when we entered her bedroom."

"Yup," added J.J. "And I'm sure glad she was okay. I felt kind of embarrassed when she kept apologizing for not being home right at ten o'clock. And then there we were going all through her house. She could have been quite upset with us for that."

"She's a wonderful lady," Henri said respectfully. "You're lucky to have such a good neighbor, J.J."

"Yes, I know. She's like a member of the family."

"What do we do now?" Mike wanted to know.

"May I use your telephone, J.J.?" Henri asked.

"Sure. What for?"

"I want to call Gramma Tessie and set up our swimming dates. Do any of you have days you would rather not swim?"

"I'd like to stay away from Sundays," J.J. volunteered.

"Me, too," added Mike. "Thursday is a bad day, too."

"I'm okay with any day," Erika added.

"I'll see what I can do. Is Tuesday or Wednesday fine with everyone?"

"Yes," they all replied.

After several minutes on the telephone with Gramma Tessie, Henri came back to the front porch. "It's all set. We can go out to swim every Tuesday at noon. Gramma Tessie said we could plan to stay as late as five o'clock if we wanted to."

"That's great! We'll have a lot of fun," exclaimed Mike. "Today's Monday. Do we start tomorrow?"

"Gramma said tomorrow would be fine if we wanted to get started on our tans right away," Henri responded. "Let's all meet at Jim's Car Wash on the north end of town. We can ride our bikes out together the first time."

Everyone agreed.

"It's almost noon. Even after several cookies, I'm still hungry," Mike admitted. It seemed like he was always hungry.

"Hey, kids," J.J.'s mom called from just inside the house. "I've got hamburgers and hot dogs on the grill, and potato salad, potato chips and dip, sweet corn, and Coke on the back patio. Anyone interested in joining me for lunch?"

A rousing "Yes" came from the porch. Mike, Henri, and Erika came inside and called home to be sure it was okay for them to stay for lunch.

J.J. stayed on the porch by himself and did some thinking. *I wonder if I should have turned back time when we entered Mrs. Montague's house,* he thought to himself. *No, I guess not. I needed to wait and see what we found first. Even if we had found her passed out or dead, if it had not happened in the past hour, I could not have helped. I guess there are some limits on what turning back time can do.*

Finally, he went inside and then out back to be with everyone else. They were sitting down all over the patio with their food. Mrs. Jamison did not tell them until after lunch that she had baked brownies for dessert.

It was nearly two o'clock when everyone was finished eating and talking. Mike said goodbye first and took the shortcut home. Erika's dad had just picked up Erika and Henri. He wanted the girls to help him with some light boxes that needed to be moved.

J.J. helped his mom clean up, and then went to his room to read. He had nothing planned and perhaps a little reading and rest would be good right now.

Jerry's door was open when he passed it. "Hi, Jer. What's up?"

"Just playing a new video game. Want to play?"

"Sure. What's it called?"

"'Monster Dragon vs. Space Invaders'. So far it's been fun. Come on in, and we can play together."

"Sounds good, thanks."

For the next two hours, the two brothers had a great time killing space invaders and saving dragons from laser light blasts.

16

DAGNAUT AND JOBLANC HAD DOWNLOADED THE recordings from Gramma Tessie's house. They were interested in what the two women had talked about a couple of days ago. They did not know who Grams was, so they hoped the recording would tell them something.

They were sure Tessie was up to something. The mentioning of the Saros stone bothered them. They listened to the recording and learned nothing. It was just two women talking about the weather, TV, and family. There were no clues about who Grams was or any secret plans the two women might have.

"We will check the recordings again in a few more days and see what they reveal. We are not making much progress," Dagnaut said disgustedly.

"You are right," added Joblanc. "We need to check for a message from our base on Jupiter's moon. We only have a week left before we need to return to Saros for treatment."

They returned to the cabin and retrieved the transmitter from under a loose board in the bedroom. There was a message for them. It stated:

"We will have a ship there to pick you up in three days. Be ready. We will pick you up at the same location as last time. We will land for only two minutes. If you are not there, we will leave without you. Be ready at 2:30 a.m. just after the moon sets. Hopefully, no one will see us. If they do, we will just look like a dark object moving like a helicopter."

Joblanc quickly sent a response confirming that they would be ready at the proper time. He did not mention Zolar.

The two men sat for a few minutes without saying anything. Then Dagnaut spoke. "We do not have much to report. We did locate Dr. M. There is the woman who mentioned a Saros stone and the young girl named Henri we are wondering about. That is all we have."

"Finding Dr. M was important. We can watch and listen to learn more about his plans when we return. We must make this place look deserted again and prepare to leave in three days," Joblanc concluded.

Three days later, at 2:30 a.m., a small ship landed in a clearing just north of the lake. Dagnaut and Joblanc hurried aboard, and it took off after being on the ground for less than a minute.

. . . .

John Grimton had been unable to sleep, so he had gone out onto his balcony overlooking the lake about 2:30 a.m. He loved astronomy and was looking up and across the lake through his binoculars. There had been a gibbous moon that cast an eerie light onto the lake. It had just dipped below the horizon.

An object suddenly came into view and passed through his field of vision. He tilted the binoculars down and focused on a dark object descending into the large clearing on the far side of the lake. This area had been prepared for a new public beach that had never been built. It made a perfect landing place. Only an overgrown rutted dirt road had been built leading to it.

He heard a low humming sound as the object landed. Then the humming became lower in pitch. He saw what looked like two figures with flashlights run to the object and disappear inside. Then the pitch rose as the object lifted off the ground.

Trying to explain what he saw would only get him laughed at. It was a ship like no other he had ever seen. He was a half mile away from it, but through his binoculars, he could see three small dots of light coming from inside it. There were no external lights. Judging by the size of the figures, the ship appeared to be about twelve feet long, eight feet wide, and seven feet tall. The ship was squarish looking with no visible wings. The ship rose straight up as it had come straight down. As it had suddenly appeared in his binoculars, it disappeared as he watched it rise above the lake. One second, it was there, and the next, it was gone.

John had seen some other strange lights in the sky over the past five years. His records were precise but lacked details. The sightings had all been at night. This was the first real object he had seen and could describe in some detail. This ship was by far the most significant of his sightings. If it appeared again, he'd report it. He'd try to get a picture next time through his telescope that was set up next to him here on his upstairs patio.

He was sure no one would believe whatever he reported. Things had happened too fast for John to look through his telescope.

....

The ship sent to pick Joblanc and Dagnaut up had a masking device. Its only shortcoming was that it required the ship to be thirty feet above the ground for it to work. Then the ship became invisible both physically and electronically. Landings and takeoffs were scheduled in the early hours of the morning and in remote areas if possible.

Dagnaut and Joblanc arrived safely on a moon orbiting Jupiter. They were transferred to a larger vessel that could travel farther and faster. Within three days, they were into and through the wormhole on their way to Saros.

It only took two hours after that to reach Saros. They had to be careful so no government ships or radar could see them arrive. General Blubick would be very angry if they were captured before giving him their report.

Their spaceship landed on the far side of Gemjah, the larger of the two moons orbiting Saros. It was a lot like Earth's moon in that it always kept the same side facing the planet it revolved around. This allowed the underground military to set up a base there. So far, it had remained undetected. A small shuttle brought Dagnaut and Joblanc to the northern region of Saros. This is where the military in opposition to the Saros government was located.

Captain Stamtu was waiting when the two spies left their shuttle and entered the space docking corridor. "Greetings. Welcome home. Follow me." He did not wait for a response and started walking toward the door to the interior of the station.

Dagnaut and Joblanc obediently followed. He led them to the medical wing where a nurse met them. "Lieutenant Jilliam will take good care of you. I will be back in two days to talk with you." He abruptly walked away.

"This way, please," ordered the lieutenant.

The two men were put through a sonic shower and then a blue laser light cleaning scan. Next, they were told to lie down on two of the six beds they came to after leaving the scanning room. A nurse in an airtight suit came up to them. He connected something to the arms of each of them. Then he pulled the transparent top down, completely enclosing the men in the cellular rejuvenation capsule. There they would remain in a sort of coma-like state while their bodies were rebuilt at a cellular level. Then they would be ready to give their report to Colonel Jabu.

Two days later, Joblanc and Dagnaut awoke. The tops of their capsules automatically opened, and the two men sat up.

"I feel great," Joblanc said.

"Me, too," reported Dagnaut. "Now, for the hard part of our mission. We have to report to Colonel Jabu."

"That is correct," said Captain Stamtu as he entered the room. "Please follow me. You can visit the cafeteria on the way to the general's office."

"The general?" gasped Joblanc.

"General Blubick has requested your presence in his office one hour after you awakened in medical. You will eat first, and then you can tell him your story."

"I never expected to see General Blubick. I hope he will not be disappointed with our report. We do not have a lot to tell him," Dagnaut stated.

"We have enough," Joblanc corrected. "We located Dr. M. We set up recording devices in his residence. We know where he works. We have not been detected and can still collect information. We have discovered Gramma Tessie who has an interest somehow in the Saros stones. I think we have done quite well."

They ate for forty-five minutes. It had been two days since they had taken any nourishment. Nothing had been needed while they were being rejuvenated. Now, they were hungry. They drank a lot of Vodrin, the preferred drink on Saros. It was made from a milky substance harvested from elogs, a creature something like the cows of Earth. Vodrin was a favorite Saronian nourishing drink.

"Time to go," ordered Captain Stamtu. He led the way down the hall to the elevator. This elevator went down five stories to the headquarters of the underground military.

The door to the general's office was open and an argument was taking place.

"I do not care what the secretary told you. I want facts, not hearsay. Now, go directly to the factory and find out why there is a delay in making more space vehicles. Here is a note my secretary wrote telling that you will report directly to me. They had better talk with you this time. Now get out of here!"

A harried young man with sergeant stripes on his sleeves came quickly through the door. He threw a quick salute to Captain Stamtu and kept right on going out of the office.

Captain Stamtu went to the doorway and saluted.

"Forget the formalities, Stamtu. Bring those guys in here."

They walked into the sparsely decorated office. The furniture consisted of five chairs clustered around a table and a desk with one large chair behind it and two armchairs in front. A watercooler, a distinct luxury, stood in one corner.

Only one wall had anything on it. There was a six-foot wide map of Earth's continents. On the round table was a similar map of Earth. There were pins sticking into the wall map, apparently marking potential landing sites for the invasion. Otherwise, the room was quite sterile looking.

"Sit down," ordered General Blubick. "Tell me everything that has happened to you since you first arrived on Earth two months ago. Leave nothing out."

Joblanc and Dagnaut spent the next hour telling everything they knew about Earth and Dr. M's mission there.

"Well done, men. I am sorry about Zolar. You handled the situation very well. You were smart to save the older woman. You covered your involvement admirably. Take five days to do whatever you want to do here, and then it is back to Earth with you. There will be no replacement for Zolar. Two of you will be less conspicuous. You have done a fine job. Get more information on this Tessie woman and her granddaughter. They might be connected to Dr. M."

"Yes, sir," both men responded.

"We are sending a contingent of thirteen soldiers to Earth in approximately four months. Their mission will be to determine where our invasion force should land. Give them any information you may have about Earth's military. Use TV reports, go online, and check on the larger bases all over the planet. We will make a plan for the full invasion force to use when they land on earth in about nine months."

The two men left the office and were returned to the surface. They were given identification tokens for military lodging on the base. That was where they would spend the next five nights.

"That went very well," Dagnaut sighed.

"See, you were worried about nothing," Joblanc responded. "I told you we had secured enough information. We should live it up for a few days and then get ready for our return to Earth."

"That sounds good to me. Right now, I am tired again. I think I will rest a little."

Their five days passed rapidly, and soon Joblanc and Dagnaut were back on that same platform, ready to be shuttled out to Gemjah. The reverse of their trip to Saros would occur, and soon they would be on Jupiter's moon, awaiting the short trip back to Earth.

A uniformed soldier approached them as they prepared to board the ship.

"I am Captain Monteford. Me and my men will accompany you to Earth. General Blubick just decided to send us back with you. You will direct us to Dr. M and tell us everything you have learned about him.

"Then we will kidnap him and any friends you point out to us. He will be forced to tell us what his plans are for Earth's defense. He will be tortured until he gives up his magno-pulse machine that he keeps on Earth.

"You must find me and my soldiers a place to stay. Our mission will last for one week. Then we will return to Saros."

Nothing unusual happened, until they landed at the base on Jupiter's moon. They were having trouble with their power generators, and a state of emergency had been declared. It was nearly two weeks before they could be returned to Earth. They wondered what had happened during the three weeks they were away.

17

DR. M'S DEPARTURE HAD BEEN KEPT SECRET AS LONG AS possible. The spacedock workers were told there were three missions being planned. None of them included Dr. M's name on the manifest. Dale and Harold were on the first ship headed for Neptune in Earth's solar system, along with two scientists and thirty soldiers. The ship's crew consisted of twenty-five members. Also aboard this ship would be Dr. M's new magno-pulse machine. It was to be packed in with other scientific equipment. It would continue on its journey to Earth either with Dale and Harold or Dr. M would pick it up from them on Neptune's moon.

The second ship carried supplies being sent to an outpost on the Saros side of the wormhole. This was a smaller ship with a crew of twelve. Fifteen soldiers accompanied them.

A third ship was going in the opposite direction to investigate a strange magnetic disturbance their satellites had detected. These were the stories being circulated around the space dock.

The supply ship would be the most likely to be attacked by the PSSG. This time, it would contain only a few supplies and a minimal crew. It was a test and a decoy.

Even though the first ship held the scientists, Dale and Harold's names were not listed anywhere. It should be safe. Even the PSSG wanted new sources of water investigated.

Sending a ship away from the wormhole had been Dr. M's idea. It presented no threat to the PSSG, and the strange anomalies near Saros needed to be investigated.

The first two ships departed without a hitch. Dale and Harold had been disguised as Saronians and taken aboard during the night shift when only one guard was present. He suspected nothing.

The science mission would test the feasibility of sending frozen water from Neptune's or Uranus' moons to Saros. Special transport ships were already being designed for this purpose.

Transporting supplies was a routine mission for the government. A small outpost was maintained near the wormhole for safety and security reasons. This base could identify any ships coming through or entering the wormhole and notify the Saros military. Help would also be nearby if any ships had an emergency. The PSSG had not interfered with the supply ships in the past. However, that could change with Dr. M's imminent return to Earth.

Dr. M was aboard the spacecraft heading to check the anomaly. He went aboard dressed as a soldier just before takeoff. Three soldiers accompanied him. The second magno-pulse machine had been loaded aboard with other equipment.

The plan was to fly for two hours toward the anomaly. Then the ship would make a wide arc and circle back to the wormhole from a totally different direction. It was hoped that it would not be noticed.

The first two hours of Dr. M's trip were routine. Nothing unusual was sighted, and soon they arrived at the coordinates where the anomaly had registered. Just as they were about to make their wide turn and head for the wormhole, a ship appeared ahead of them. It looked like one of their ships and was drifting near a small asteroid.

"We had better check this out," Captain Bonner said. "Take us in slowly, helmsman."

A minute later, the helmsman called out, "One hundred meters, Captain."

"Hold us here," Captain Bonner ordered.

Light could be seen coming from six small windows along the side of the ship. There was a clear canopy at the front, but no light shone from it.

"Can we dock with it?" the Captain asked.

"Yes," replied the helmsman.

"Then do so."

Slowly, the distance between the two ships diminished. The docking ports lined up, and they were connected.

Captain Bonner led the boarding party of three through the airlock and into the other ship. The air had registered as safe to breathe, so air packs were not needed.

The two ships were nearly identical. "This is definitely one of our ships," Captain Bonner stated. "What is it doing clear out here?"

"I can answer that," came the voice of a soldier who stepped from around a corner. Three others appeared, and they had weapons aimed at the boarding party.

"Remove your weapons slowly and place them on the floor. We are not here to hurt anyone. We will go back to your ship, get what we came for, and then you can continue your mission. The anomaly you saw was a ruse to get you out here."

"What do you want?" Captain Bonner asked, getting more perturbed by the minute.

"That does not concern you. Follow my soldiers and do not do anything stupid. No one will be injured if you do as I say. I will be right behind with my weapon pointed at your back."

They walked back through the airlock. Once aboard the government ship, the man identified himself.

"I am Captain Stamtu of the PSSG. Please take me to Dr. M."

"Dr. M is not aboard this vessel," stated Captain Bonner.

"I know he is here!" shouted an angry Captain Stamtu. He aimed his weapon at one of the government soldiers and fired. A blue light flashed out along with a loud buzz. The soldier crumpled to the floor, stunned and paralyzed. "The next shot will not be to paralyze," he said as he adjusted the setting on his weapon. "Now, take me to Dr. M."

"Okay. You win. Follow me."

They walked down a short hall and entered an elevator. It took them down two levels. Once again, in a hallway, Captain Bonner said, "It is the second door on the right."

They all walked to Dr. M's door, and Captain Bonner pushed the button on the wall.

"Yes?" came Dr. M's voice from within. "Who is it?"

Captain Stamtu jabbed his weapon into Captain Bonner's back.

"Captain Bonner. May I come in? It's important."

A swooshing sound was heard as the door slid into the wall. Captain Bonner was pushed into the room, and Captain Stamtu and two of his soldiers followed.

"What's the meaning of this? You're interfering with a government mission," Dr. M stated emphatically. "Get off our ship!"

"Calm down, Dr. M. You are in no position to give orders. All we want is the magno-pulse."

"It's not here. How did you know I was here?"

"Remember your conversation with Colonel Jabu? We have spies and supporters everywhere. Information was relayed to us describing all three of the government's missions. We know about the mission to Neptune and

Uranus to determine if the frozen water is potable and could be transported to Saros.

"We also know the details about the mission carrying limited supplies to the outpost near the wormhole. And finally, we have the best information of all. We know that you are traveling back to Earth disguised as a soldier. We also know that you brought the magno-pulse machine along packaged with some other equipment. Was this clever plan yours?"

"Yes, but it wasn't clever enough."

"Now, give us the magno-pulse machine or we will tear the ship apart searching for it. My orders are to let you continue to Earth if you give us the machine. If you resist, I am authorized to use deadly force and even destroy your ship and everyone on it."

"You leave me no choice."

"That is the idea."

"It's in a large box with the other supplies in the cargo bay. I can take you to it."

"Lead the way. We have two other ships on the other side of the asteroid. Their orders are to destroy your ship if we do not contact them in one hour. So do not try anything."

"I won't endanger the crew of this ship. The magno-pulse is in a briefcase-like satchel. It is protected by an acid lock system. Only I have the correct combination. Follow me."

They left the room and went to the elevator. Two of the PSSG troops went first to secure the cargo bay. Then

Captain Stamtu, Dr. M, and the remaining soldier followed.

Once there, Dr. M identified the proper container. Two soldiers pried it open and found the satchel. Carefully, Dr. M worked the combination and opened the case. He pulled the magno-pulse machine out and handed it to Captain Stamtu.

"Here it is. This is the new version. As I told Colonel Jabu, I am not sure it works. My system may be immune to Earth's yellow sun's deadly rays."

"We will decide that." Captain Stamtu turned to his soldiers. "Tie them up. We are leaving now. We will honor our word. You are free to continue your mission." He pulled out his radio and contacted his other two ships. "Your ship now has the weapons of our two ships aimed at it. Captain, contact your bridge and order them to allow us to depart safely."

Captain Bonner took the communicator Captain Stamtu offered him. "Bridge, this is the captain. There are two enemy vessels with weapons trained on us. Do not take any action. The vessel we are docked with is about to depart. Allow all three ships to move away from us."

"Orders received and understood, Captain," responded the second in command from the bridge.

They bound Captain Bonner, Dr. M, and the two soldiers and left through the airlock connecting the two ships. Then they broke the connection. Slowly, the PSSG ship moved away. When it was safely away, it suddenly started to glow and disappeared in a streak of white light. The other two ships did the same.

A few minutes later, a soldier entered the cargo bay. He untied the four men and stepped back, waiting for orders.

"We must get to the bridge," ordered Captain Bonner. "How serious is the loss of the magno-pulse machine?"

"It's a huge loss," Dr. M replied. "If it works for them, they will be able to invade Earth within six months and stay there indefinitely."

"What can we do to stop them?"

"Nothing. Let's get on with our mission to get me back to Earth. There is much to be done."

Captain Bonner and the soldiers entered the elevator and rode up to the bridge. "Helmsman, take us to the wormhole. Fastest available speed."

"Aye, aye, sir," replied the helmsman. "It will take us four hours to get to the wormhole."

"Stay alert, men. We were just surprised and outmaneuvered by the enemy. We are fortunate they decided to be friendly. Stay vigilant. There may be more surprises ahead of us."

In his quarters, Dr. M smiled as he thought, *It will take them two months using the machine they stole to determine it does not work. They will never know they have the one with the defective parts. I hope no one dies because of my deception. At least, they didn't get the real enhanced magno-pulse.*

Just under four hours later, the helmsman spoke to Captain Bonner. "Sir, we are approaching the wormhole. Should I order everyone to their on-duty stations?"

"Yes. Issue the order."

Within minutes, everyone was either in his quarters or at his on-duty station. It was usually a bumpy ride through the wormhole. They needed to be prepared.

They traveled through the wormhole and entered Earth's solar system. There was no sign of their other ship. "Perhaps they have already landed on Triton, one of the moons orbiting Neptune, and already started their research," Captain Bonner stated.

I do not want a war, Dr. M thought. *But that is what is about to happen. The PSSG will use the magno-pulse machine on some of their people. In two months, they will discover that it is not protecting them from the yellow sun's deadly rays. That is when things will get very interesting.*

18

THE SUMMER WAS PASSING QUICKLY FOR THE KIDS OF Millville. Three trips to Gramma Tessie's to swim provided a nice break in the routine. Henri and Erika had called Ann who was visiting at the lake. Joey had been included in the swimming activities so he and Freddie could entertain each other.

Ann became good friends with Henri and Erika. She began to wish she did not have to return home in six weeks. Her parents had several family events planned for early August, so she and Freddie had to go home. Perhaps they could arrange visits during school holidays.

Her family lived on a small fishing lake. She didn't care for fishing, but Freddie liked it. He and Dad usually went out once a week. Of course, that changed while they were staying with their grandmother.

The big Fourth of July weekend was a week away. Everyone was talking about the fireworks scheduled for Friday evening.

Henri and her mom were having lunch at Gramma Tessie's place.

"Why don't you invite your friends out for a Fourth of July swim and picnic?" Gramma Tessie asked Henri. "They could spend the afternoon here and go back to town for the fireworks."

"That's a great idea. Thanks, Gramma," Henri replied.

"I'll help with the preparations," Henri's mom added. "I'll call Erika, Mike, and J.J.'s moms to see if they will help also. Then it won't be so much work for Gramma."

"Thanks," Gramma Tessie said. "This will be a party to remember."

They finished lunch and drove back to town. Henri read for a while and finished her library book.

"May I walk to the library and return my book, Mom? I'd like to look for something new to read."

"Sure," Mrs. Matthews replied.

"Is it okay if I walk down to Deano's when I finish at the library?"

"Okay. Call me when you are ready to come home, and I'll pick you up at Deano's."

"It's 4:30 now. I'll probably be ready around eight o'clock."

Henri had not used her power over time in three weeks. Sometimes she forgot she was even wearing the necklace. When she least expected it, time would reveal a need for her power. That time was an hour away.

J.J. had signed up for the algebra class at the library with Erika. It had gone well. They studied together before the class each week. They used computers in the community room at the library. There was one session remaining in the four-week class. Both kids would be glad when it was finished.

J.J. was thinking to himself as he was walking to the library. It was only five blocks from his house. Erika would walk six blocks coming from another direction. It was 4:30, and the class would start at five o'clock. It would be finished at six o'clock, and he would be free for the rest of the summer.

I wonder if my power still works, he thought as he walked along the sidewalk in the shade of a large oak tree. *I haven't used it in nearly three weeks. Can I still turn back time?* he wondered. *I sure wish I could talk with someone about this.*

He arrived at the library to find Erika sitting outside, waiting for him. They went in together. J.J. liked Erika but only as a friend. They had talked about it and Erika felt the same way about him.

"Want to stop by Deano's with me for a soda?" he asked Erika as they left the library an hour later.

"I'd like to, but my dad is picking me up. There he is now. I have to babysit my little brother while my parents go to a big dinner."

"Hey!" came a familiar voice from just inside the library. "Wait up, you guys. Mind if I join you?"

"Hey, Henri," returned J.J.

"Hi, Henri," replied Erika. "What are you doing here?"

"I just got a couple of books about time travel and the universe."

"What for?" asked Erika curiously. "That's weird stuff."

"I like space stories," J.J. chimed in. "*Star Trek* is my favorite."

"I'm just reading for fun. The universe is really big. There could be life in other parts of it."

"Let me know if you find anything good," added J.J. "I'm going to Deano's. Want to come along?"

"Sure. You coming, Erika?" asked Henri.

"No. I wish I could. I'm babysitting in a few minutes. That's our car pulling up. Do you guys want a ride? Deano's is ten blocks away. I'm sure my dad wouldn't mind swinging around that way."

"Sure," answered both J.J. and Henri.

They had driven a few blocks when Henri got that uneasy feeling again. *I feel like I'm being warned about another opportunity to stop time and avoid a disaster,* she thought.

J.J. was sitting with Henri in the backseat. *What is this strange feeling I have?* he thought. *I feel something terrible is about to happen. Why am I thinking this?* His wrist was getting warm where the bracelet was. *What should I do?* he wondered.

His unspoken question was answered in the next instant. Mr. Sorenson had just pulled away from the stop sign and was crossing the intersection when a bright red truck came flying past the stop sign on their right. It raced past behind them, barely missing their car.

Henri had seen the truck coming. The back of the red truck had just passed behind them when she got her necklace out and pressed her thumbs into it.

When she looked around, she saw a man in the crosswalk right in front of the truck. His dog was a couple of feet in front of him on an extendable leash. The truck was about to hit them both when it was frozen in time just short of the crosswalk.

They will be killed when time starts again, she thought. *What can I do? If I touch the man to move him, he will wake up and see what is happening. I can't do that.*

Henri put the necklace back inside her shirt. Then, she reached down with her left hand to push herself up from the seat and out the door. She brushed J.J.'s arm. Instantly, he was awake. He looked around.

"What's going on? That truck ran the stop sign and just missed us, I think. The car has stopped and so has the truck. Why isn't anyone moving? Henri, what's happening?"

"I don't know how to explain it, but please don't touch anyone. If you do, they might wake up, too."

"Wake up from what? Why are they asleep?"

"They're not asleep. Oh, my gosh! What have I done?" she hesitated for a moment and then added, "They're suspended in time."

"They're suspended in time? That's impossible. Why are you and I the only ones talking and moving?"

"Because I accidentally touched you. You woke up because I touched your arm when I was trying to get out of the car. What's that bracelet on your wrist? Where did you get it?"

"What bracelet?"

"That one." She reached out and touched it. "It's warm. Where did you get it?"

"How can you see my bracelet? No one can see it."

"I don't know why I can see it." She reached inside her blouse and pulled out her necklace.

"That stone looks just like mine!" an astonished J.J. exclaimed. "Where did you get it?"

"Wait. You can see my necklace? No one is supposed to be able to see it. How can you see it?"

"I don't know. Maybe the same way you can see my bracelet. Now, where did you get it?" he demanded.

"I asked you first."

"It was a gift from a friend."

"So was mine. What kind of friend?"

"I'm not supposed to tell."

"Me neither."

"Then maybe we better not."

"Does your bracelet give you any special power?" Henri continued her questions.

"Why do you ask that?"

"Take a look around you. Isn't this a little strange?"

"It's a lot strange! Did you do this? Did you freeze everyone, everything?"

"They're suspended in time. You didn't answer my question. What does your bracelet do? It must have something to do with time."

"I'm not supposed to tell anyone."

"I wasn't supposed to tell you about my power either, but I did. How are we going to save that man and his dog? Can you do something?"

"Okay. Maybe it's meant to be. I've been wishing I had someone to talk to about this bracelet. You must be the one."

"Talk to me then," Henri said impatiently.

"You're not going to believe this."

"Do you believe what you are seeing now?"

"Okay, okay. My bracelet can turn time back one hour. Then everything happens again unless I do something to change it."

"Do you remember that things are happening again?"

"Yes. I'm the only one who knows things are being relived. I've done it twice."

"So you can turn time back to before this happened?"

"Yes, I guess I could," he said slowly, still staring at the motionless man and his dog. "But what about your necklace? How does it work?"

"I press my thumbs together on both sides of the stone. Time stands still for an hour. I am the only one who can move. Anyone I touch comes awake. This is the third time I've made time stand still."

"Wow!" said J.J., finally beginning to understand what was happening. "We have similar powers. I feel good being able to talk about it."

"Me, too," Henri added with a smile. "What are we going to do about this accident that is about to happen?"

"I don't know. Let's think about it for a minute. If you touch the man, he will wake up and know about your power. There's nothing we can do about the truck. It's too close to the man."

"I don't know if my bracelet can turn time back while it is suspended. That would be a good start." J.J. was thinking about what they could do if time turned back to an hour ago. "We would all be back at the library. How could we save the man and his dog then?"

Henri had an answer. "We would have to get to this intersection sooner. Then we could somehow warn the man. We could try to stop him from crossing the street until the red truck goes past."

"That's a good plan. We will have to jump right into Mr. Sorenson's car and make an excuse for him to drive a little faster than he did the first time. We'll think of something."

"Go ahead. Try it. Will I remember what has happened when you turn time back?"

"I don't think so. No one has noticed when I turned time back before and made some changes."

"I don't want to forget about your power. Then I'll be alone again," Henri added sadly.

"Don't worry. I'll tell you."

"Then turn time back."

J.J. hesitated for several seconds. "Okay. Here goes." He placed his right thumb onto the stone.

19

NOTHING HAPPENED!

"My power won't work while time is suspended," J.J. said with a sigh.

"Then what can we do? If I start time up again, you might not be able to turn time back before the truck hits that man and his dog. We would have to watch them get killed. That would be awful."

"Wait. I have an idea. When time is relived, no one reliving it knows it is being relived. I think we can wake him up, have him and his dog move back to safety, and then start time again. Then I can send time back an hour, and we can relive it. Only this time, we'll stop the man before he crosses the street. He won't remember that he saw everything frozen or that he talked with us."

"Let's think about this," Henri suggested. They sat down on the curb to think. This was a difficult problem.

After a few minutes, Henri added, "We only have an hour before time starts again on its own. There must be some way to make it work out so the man and his dog are saved and we're not discovered."

"I can't think of any other way to do it. You touch the man. When he wakes up, I'll say, 'Sir, pick up your dog and carry him back to the sidewalk. I know you don't believe this, but time has been stopped, frozen in place. This red truck is about to hit you and your dog. This will save your lives. Please don't ask any questions. Just do as I say.' After they are safely on the sidewalk, you start time again. We don't even have to get back in the car."

"Then Erika and her dad will wonder how we got out of the car and over here."

"That won't matter because when I turn time back an hour, they won't remember any of this."

"That might work," Henri said, getting a little excited. "How do we keep the man from crossing the street?"

"We'll have about forty-five minutes to work on that. I think your idea of getting right into the car and asking Mr. Sorenson to hurry a little bit will work. We have to get to this intersection sooner than we just did. If we can get here early enough, we can have him pull over. We can tell him we need to stop at that convenience store over there or I could pretend to be sick. He'd stop to let me out to throw up, I'm sure."

"Then we call to the man and run over to try to slow him down enough for the truck to drive past and miss him."

They thought about it a little more and decided that this was the best plan they could devise. So they got up and proceeded with it.

Henri touched the man on the shoulder. He was startled but continued what he had been about to do. "Noooooooo!" he screamed as he had seen the red truck about to crash into them. Then he noticed that the truck was not moving. Neither was his dog. "Benji, come here, boy." The dog did not move.

Then the man noticed the two kids standing right behind him. "Who are you? Why doesn't Benji move? Why is the truck stopped? What's going on?"

"Calm down, sir," J.J. pleaded. "Pick up your dog and carry him back to the sidewalk. I know you don't believe this, but time has been stopped, frozen in place. That red truck is about to hit you and your dog. This will save your lives. Please do not ask any questions. Just do as I say. Get yourselves out from in front of that truck."

"This cannot be happening. Are we dead?"

"No, sir. You're awake," responded Henri. "Please pick up your dog and move to safety."

He picked up his dog. Luckily, it was a small dog. Once they were safely on the sidewalk, Henri pressed the stone on her necklace. The red truck rushed past and continued down the street. "Rarf, rarf," the dog barked at the kids.

The man held his dog tightly as he wiped his eyes. He had tears running down his cheeks. In a shaky voice, he said, "I lost my wife three months ago to cancer. I rescued this dog from the pound last week. We're just getting to know each other. He's been a wonderful companion so far. I couldn't bear to lose him."

"We're so sorry about your wife," Henri responded. "What a cute little dog."

"I don't understand what happened. You saved our lives. How can I ever thank you?"

"You just did," remarked Henri.

And then J.J. touched his bracelet.

The next thing Henri and J.J. knew, they were back in the library. J.J. checked the wall clock to see that it was twenty minutes after five. He had turned back time. When class finished in forty minutes, he and Henri wouldn't have much time left in which to save the man and his dog.

Henri found herself back inside the library, too. She was looking at books on the shelf in the science section. She wanted one about the universe. Then she remembered what had just happened to J.J. and her.

J.J. and Erika's class finished at six o'clock just like before. "Want to stop by Deano's with me for a soda?" J.J. asked as they walked out of the library.

"I'd like to, but my dad is picking me up. There he is now. I have to babysit my little brother while my parents go to a big dinner."

"Hey!" came a familiar voice from just inside the library. "Wait up, you guys. Mind if I join you?"

"Hey, Henri," returned J.J.

"Hi, Henri," replied Erika "What are you doing here?"

"I just got a couple of books about time travel and the universe."

"What for?" asked Erika curiously. "That's weird stuff."

"I like space stories," J.J. chimed in. "*Star Trek* is my favorite."

"I'm just reading for fun. The universe is really big. There could be life in other parts of it."

"Let me know if you find anything good," added J.J. "I'm going to Deano's. Want to come along?"

Henri looked at J.J. and winked. "Sure."

She knows, he thought as a smile crossed his face. *She remembers our stopping time and turning it back. We have to get to that intersection and save that man and his dog.*

Henri smiled back at J.J. and turned to Erika, "Are you coming?"

"No, I wish I could. I'm babysitting in a few minutes. That's our car pulling up. Do you guys want a ride? Deano's is ten blocks away. I'm sure my dad wouldn't mind swinging around that way."

"Sure," answered both J.J. and Henri as they quickly walked over to Mr. Sorenson's car. They were in a hurry to get back to that intersection.

After a few minutes in the car, J.J. thought, *We have to get to that intersection faster than before. What should I do?*

"Mr. Sorenson," said Henri, "I hate to ask this, but could you go just a little faster? I really have to go to the bathroom. I should have used the facilities at the library. I'm sorry."

"Sure. No problem. I understand," he replied. He sped up just a little.

This should be enough to get us there a couple of minutes before the truck runs the stop sign, thought Henri.

It's going to be close, feared J.J.

They had driven a few more blocks when Henri and J.J. got that uneasy feeling again. They knew what was about to happen as they approached the critical intersection.

"Mr. Sorenson, please pull into that parking lot!" shouted J.J. "I think I'm going to throw up."

Mr. Sorenson pulled into the parking lot at the corner convenience store. This was the intersection. Henri and J.J. saw the elderly man and his dog walk to the corner. They stopped before crossing.

Oh, no! Henri thought. She looked to the right and saw the red truck coming. Quickly, both she and J.J. opened their doors and got out. They ran to the corner and yelled across the street to the man. "Hey, mister, wait a minute. Don't cross. Please wait."

The man had already started across the street in the crosswalk. He was nearly halfway across when he heard the shouts. His dog barked and pulled ahead. The man was startled. He stopped and his fingers tightened on the retractable leash. He accidentally released the lock and the dog went ahead a few feet right into the path of the red truck.

The red truck raced through the stop sign and struck the dog. The impact pulled the leash from the man's hand. The dog was hit by something under the truck and was dragged along with it. Then he fell free and lay motionless in the street.

"Noooooooo!" screamed the man.

Two teens were in the truck. Realizing they had struck something, the driver slammed on the brakes and pulled to the side of the street. He was devastated when he saw the blood stains on the pavement behind his truck. He felt sick to his stomach when he saw the dead dog lying in the street some twenty feet behind his truck. Then he saw the man and the two kids coming toward him.

"Oh, no. My poor Benji," sobbed the elderly man. Tears were streaming down his face as he lifted the dead dog up and held him to his chest. "How could this happen?"

"I'm so sorry, sir. I didn't see him," the driver of the truck said.

"We had better call the police," stated Mr. Sorenson. He had followed them and was taking out his cell phone.

"What will I do?" cried the man. "First, my wife of fifty-six years, and now, my Benji. I'm all alone again."

Mr. Sorenson put an arm around the man and tried to console him. "We'll stay with you, sir. You can count on us."

"That's right," added Henri. "We're so glad you were not injured."

The man looked at Henri and said, "Were you the one who yelled at me? I would have been out there with Benji if you hadn't hollered at me. What made you do that? You saved my life."

Thinking quickly, Henri responded, "Your dog was so cute. He looked just like the one a friend of mine had back in Detroit. It's a rare breed, and I thought your dog might be the same. I wanted to get a closer look at it. I didn't know there were any Papillons here in Millville. Oh, I'm so sorry about your dog."

"It's not your fault. I rescued Benji from the pound last week. We were just getting to know each other. He's been a wonderful companion."

The police arrived a few minutes later. The truck driver admitted he was texting when he ran the stop sign and hit the dog. After checking the license, registration, and insurance, the eighteen-year-old driver was issued a citation.

"Be sure you tell your parents what happened," the officer instructed. "You are very lucky you didn't kill someone today."

The teen was very contrite and realized how serious the situation was. "I know, sir. I am very sorry about your dog, mister. I would like to make restitution. I've written my name and telephone number on this paper. Call when you are ready, and I will pay to get you another dog."

"Dr. Hollister is a friend of mine," Mr. Sorenson said. "He runs the veterinary clinic on the edge of town. Would you like me to call him? He can help you with Benji."

"That's very nice of both of you," replied the elderly gentleman. He took the slip of paper from the young man. "Please be more careful when driving," he told the young man.

"Yes, sir, I promise," replied the still shaken truck driver. He and his friend walked over to the truck and drove off, slowly.

"I don't want to be any trouble," the man continued.

"We'll be glad to help," Henri added. "You must live nearby. Can we give you a ride home? Do you have any family here?"

"I live two blocks over on Center Street. It's 203 South Center Street. I live alone, but my son's family lives a few blocks away. I suppose we should call him. His name is Nick Cole. He's a policeman. Perhaps you know him, Officer."

"Yes, I do. We work out of the same office. I think he's on duty now. I'll call him for you."

"Thank you. My grandchildren are going to be very sad about this. Sammy and Kati were thrilled when I got Benji."

"Is Sammy in the fifth grade by any chance?" asked J.J.

"Yes. He had a scare just before school let out for the summer. He collapsed while running a race. Luckily, the school nurse was there. She saved his life. How am I going to explain this to him and his sister?"

This is Sammy's grandfather, thought J.J. *Wow! I was a part of saving Sammy and his grandfather. What a coincidence. But this didn't turn out as we had planned. The dog was killed. I guess we can't predict how things will turn out when we repeat time.* J.J. was concerned about this turn of events.

"We'd be happy to help you find another dog," Henri offered.

"That's very nice of you. Let's wait a while before I think about getting another dog. Perhaps the vet will have an idea about what's available for adoption. I could go to the pound again. I need some time to think about this."

Just then Officer Cole arrived in his patrol car. Flares had been placed around the blood in the street. Pictures had been taken, as well as statements from the witnesses. The police work was just about finished.

"Dad! Are you all right?" Officer Cole asked, concern sounding in his voice. "What happened?"

"I'm fine but very sad. Benji has been killed. A truck ran the stop sign and hit him. It barely missed me. If this young lady hadn't called to me just before the accident, I could be dead, too. She saved my life."

"Is that true, young lady?" asked Officer Cole.

"I guess so," replied Henri. "I only wanted to ask him about his dog. Oh, I feel so bad for your father. He told us about your mother."

"Dad has had a rough few months. We were happy for him when he adopted Benji. He started to live again. And now, another tragedy has happened. I don't know what he'll do."

"We called Dr. Hollister," Mr. Sorenson said. "He's a friend who runs the vet clinic. He's on his way to get Benji."

"You people have been very kind," Officer Cole said.

The vet arrived a few minutes later and carefully wrapped Benji in a blanket. Grandpa Cole gave him his telephone number, and Dr. Hollister said he would call tomorrow.

"Thanks for helping," Officer Cole added. "I should get Dad home now."

Then Mr. Sorenson drove the kids to Deano's. "Thanks for the ride, Mr. Sorenson," said J.J. "I need to get right inside."

"Bye, Erika," Henri said as she closed the car door. She went inside to get a booth and wait for J.J.

20

J.J. CAME OUT OF THE BATHROOM AND SAT ACROSS FROM Henri. They looked at each other for a couple of minutes, saying nothing.

Henri finally broke the silence. "This has been quite an evening. I was told not to talk about my gift to anyone, and I told you. You were told the same thing, and you told me."

"We should find a safer place to discuss this. Someone might hear us if we talk in such a public place," J.J. stated.

"I agree. Why don't we go out to see Gramma Tessie in the morning and talk?"

"I was about to suggest we go to see Grams to talk. Either place would be okay. We just need to get away from people."

Henri's cell phone rang. "Hello?" she answered.

"Hi, Henri. It's Gramma Tessie. Would you and J.J. like to come out tomorrow? I have something quite interesting to tell both of you."

"Hold on a minute, please," she requested. "It's Gramma Tessie. She wants us to come out tomorrow. She has something interesting to tell us. How strange she should call just as we were talking about her."

"Tell her yes. Ask her what time."

"Gramma? Sure we can come out tomorrow. What time should we be there?"

"Come out at eleven o'clock. Plan to stay two to three hours."

"Okay, we'll be there. Bye."

"What time did she say?"

"She said to come at eleven o'clock and plan to stay two to three hours. Should we order something?"

"I'm not hungry anymore," J.J. announced. "Gramma Tessie's call has me worried. I wonder what she wants."

"We'll find out tomorrow. I'll call my mom to pick us up," Henri offered. "She said to call when I was ready to come home. She knew I might walk over to Deano's after visiting the library."

"Will she mind dropping me off at my house?"

"No. We can tell her about Gramma's call and her invitation."

"Okay, I'll ask my mom when I get home. I'll call and let you know what she says."

Henri's mom picked them up ten minutes later.

"Mom, Gramma Tessie wants J.J. and me to come out to her house tomorrow morning. Is that okay with you? We can ride our bikes. She wants us to be there at eleven o'clock and said we'd be there until around two."

"Sure, that's fine with me."

When J.J. got home, he asked his mother about the trip to Gramma Tessie's, and she said yes. So it was set.

Henri and J.J. had talked before Mrs. Matthews picked them up. Their houses weren't too far apart, so they had planned to meet about thirty minutes later at eight o'clock. There was a small park and playground halfway between their houses.

"Hi, again," J.J. said with a friendly smile as they met near a picnic table in the park.

"Hi," came Henri's reply. "Let's sit at this table."

"Okay." There were a few kids playing on the toys and swings nearby. Their parents were sitting in lawn chairs watching them play.

"I don't think anyone can hear us," J.J. stated. He got right to the point. "Now, where did you get your necklace?"

"You must promise not to tell anyone. You must also promise to tell me where you got your bracelet."

"Okay, I promise."

"My necklace came from Gramma Tessie. She said it had been handed down for generations, but that only every third generation could use its power."

"Did she say why she gave it to you?"

"Yes. She said both she and my mother were the skipped generations. The necklace had been vibrating recently when she held it, and she took that as a sign that it was time to give it to me. I was the 'chosen one' is what the necklace told me when I activated its power."

"This is really strange. My bracelet told me the same thing."

"Where did you get your bracelet?" Henri asked impatiently. She really wanted to know.

"I found a letter in an old Bible that belonged to Great-grandpa Jamison. It was addressed to the first son of his first son's first son. That's me. So it skipped two generations just like your necklace did. I don't get it."

"I don't either. Why us? What are we supposed to do with these powers? How will we know when to use them?"

"Grams surprised me a week ago when she asked me out for a visit. She said she knew all about the bracelet and its power. She said there were special things ahead for me to do. She said there was someone else who had a power similar to mine and that I would be meeting that person soon. How could she know these things?"

"I don't know. I think Gramma Tessie knows more than she has been telling me, too."

"I know one thing, Henri. It's a relief to be able to talk to someone about what is going on. I hated to have to keep what I was doing a secret."

"Me, too. But we will have to be very careful not to be overheard when we talk."

"Grams also told me there were three people who knew about my power. One of them is a leader who will help us use our powers. She said I would meet this person either by the end of the summer or in the early fall."

"Do you think Gramma Tessie wants to talk with us about our powers tomorrow?" Henri asked.

"Probably. Tell me what you have used your power for so far."

"Okay," Henri replied, thankful that she had someone to talk to. For the next hour, they exchanged stories about their recent adventures with time. It was nine o'clock and starting to get dark when they agreed it was time to go home.

"See you back here at 10:30 in the morning," J.J. said as they went their separate ways.

"Okay. It will be interesting to hear what Gramma has to say to us. Won't she be surprised when we tell her we know about each other's power?"

"Nothing will surprise me anymore. See you tomorrow. Good night." *Tomorrow will be a special day for sure. Maybe Gramma Tessie can answer some of our questions about why we were given these stones,* he thought.

21

THEY ORBITED NEPTUNE AND DOCKED WITH THE OTHER SHIP. The scientists were already hard at work. Dr. M retrieved his enhanced magno-pulse machine. Then they proceeded on to the Earth's moon. They made their approach to the dark side of the moon during a new moon cycle and landed without anyone on Earth noticing. Even the PSSG base on Ganymede did not notice their arrival.

Later that night, Dr. M was delivered to Earth, landing unseen in a desolate area twenty miles northeast of Millville. Major Stromberg was there to meet him.

"Welcome back, Dr. M," stated the major with a strict military bearing. "What did you learn?"

"It's good to be back. Earth feels so much more like home to me now. I have lots of news. First, the radical military on Saros is sending a ship with thirteen people aboard to Earth sometime in the next few months. Their mission is to search for and determine landing sites for the invasion. The invasion is scheduled for eight to nine months from now."

"What should we do?"

"Nothing. Let's wait and see what happens in the next few months. We have a highly trained spy we think is being included in the preliminary landing group. He will keep us informed of their plans once they land. There might be a way to sabotage their efforts. Perhaps we can even capture them so no intelligence reports get back to Saros. On an even more positive note, we might be able to send back our own messages to their headquarters."

"How would we accomplish that?"

"Let me work on it for a few weeks. I will know a lot more once their ship lands here. Then we will hear from Captain Lothu with his evaluation. I will keep you informed."

"The president is not going to like this invasion news."

"Don't tell him. He might panic. The forces from Saros might be small, but they are formidable. In the worst case, we will have to send government military ships here to fight the underground military. I hope that doesn't happen. If we can thwart their preliminary plans, we might be able to stop the invasion."

"Are you sure about all of this?"

"Yes. Earth's defenses at present would be no match for the seven-ship invasion force. They would cause incredible damage. All they want is the water, so any land damage or human deaths would not concern them. They can only stay here for two months before having to return to Saros for regeneration treatments. That will work in our favor."

"Okay. I can give you three months. You must convince me in that time that you can stop the invasion. Then I must inform the president."

"Fair enough. Now, get me home so I can start to work on saving two planets."

"What do you mean, saving two planets?"

"Earth is in danger of being destroyed by an invasion, and Saros will die for lack of water. I have an idea how to solve both problems."

"Care to enlighten me?"

"Not presently. I will fill you in as my plan unfolds."

Major Stromberg opened the door to the black Lincoln Town Car, and they got in. They drove off quietly in the direction of Millville. The other two Town Cars followed.

After dropping Dr. M off at a friend's house six miles north of Millville, Major Stromberg and his contingent drove north for several hours to a military base. From there, he would be flown back to Washington, D.C.

Dr. M had left his car here at his friend's house. He got into his car and drove home. He was already wondering what the surveillance tapes at his house would show.

It was nearly midnight when Dr. M arrived back home. His house was in a pleasant neighborhood just a mile from town in a small subdivision. He stopped in the driveway, opened the garage door, and pulled inside. He waited until the garage door was closed before getting out of his car.

There was a special concealed compartment under the third row of seats in his sports utility vehicle. He had hidden the enhanced magno-pulse machine there. He removed it and locked it inside a wall cabinet. Then he went into the house. He would come out in an hour to move the truck. There was a concealed compartment in the garage floor. He would secure the magno-pulse machine there and park the SUV over it.

Once inside, he checked to see if anything had been disturbed. Everything looked okay. Then he thought, *Now, I'll have a look at the security recordings to see if anyone has been in here.* He went into the bedroom closet and disabled the special alarm. Then he pushed a hidden lever, and a small door opened in the back of the closet. He stepped into a six foot by four foot size room that became illuminated when he pushed the light switch. As the lights came on, the door to the room closed.

This room was a lot like the electronics room at Gram's farm but much smaller. Dr. M had brought upgraded equipment from Saros when he first started coming to Earth.

He looked at the external recording first. The cameras recorded using night vision technology. He could easily see the older model car parked in front of his house. He watched as three men exited the car and approached his front door. *I wonder who they are* he thought. He saw them knock on the door and then walk around the side of the house. Another camera picked them up as they came to the back of the house and entered through a window. *This is interesting. I wonder what they are looking for.*

He switched to the interior surveillance recording next. His thoughts were interrupted when one of the men spoke.

"You two check the kitchen. I will check the next room," he heard someone say. "Search his cabinets and decide where to put the recorders."

Another of the intruders shouted, "Look what I found: two one-hundred-dollar bills, three twenties, a five, and six ones in the cookie jar inside a cupboard."

The first man replied, "I can use them in the replicator to make more U.S. currency."

More conversation met Dr. M's listening ears. "I think we should put one inside that register in the wall."

"I will do that," one of the men answered.

"Joblanc, look around the other rooms and see if he has an office," the man who seemed to be in charge had ordered.

"No office. Just three bedrooms and two bathrooms." One of the men reported.

"Then we will put the other recorder in the ceiling vent in the kitchen. Aim it at the table, Zolar."

"When did you say Dr. M was returning from Saros?" asked one of the men.

"Not for a couple of weeks. Get that last recorder installed so we can get out of here. Then we can listen to Dr. M from half a mile away. Hopefully, he will say something that will tell us what his plans are. General Blubick is counting on us. We might get a promotion if we do well on this assignment."

"That would be great!" one of the men said. "Dr. M will never know we were in his house. Good job, men."

"So these three are the military men sent from Saros to spy on Earth," Dr. M stated stoically. "I will need to think about this and decide how to handle this new development."

He listened a little more, and deciding there was nothing more to be learned, he reset his security recorders. Then he pushed the button to turn off the lights. The door opened, he exited through it, and pushed the lever to close the hidden door panel. He carefully arranged the clothes on the rack to cover the door and placed a box and a pair of shoes on the floor in front of the hidden door.

He was very tired from his long trip and a good night's sleep was just what he needed.

First, he went to the garage, backed the car out, and closed the garage door. Then he went into the house and entered the garage through the side door. Activating the switch that controlled the hidden compartment in the garage floor, he stood back and watched. The concrete split apart to reveal a four by six by two foot open space. He retrieved the magno-pulse from the locked cabinet and placed it in the open floor space. Then he pushed the switch again and the floor closed, concealing the magno-pulse.

Finally, he went through the house and came out the front door. He opened the garage door from inside his truck and pulled the SUV into the garage. After closing the garage door, he went into the house to a long anticipated sleep in his favorite bed.

22

THE NEXT MORNING, BOTH J.J. AND HENRI WERE UP EARLY. They were very nervous about their meeting with Gramma Tessie at eleven o'clock.

What am I doing? J.J. thought to himself at eight o'clock. *I've been up for an hour, and all I've done is clean, clean, clean. I've rearranged all the furniture. Everything is picked up and put away. There's nothing left to do, and I have all this energy.*

He came bounding down the stairs to find Mom in the kitchen.

"Breakfast is ready," she announced.

"How did you know I was up?"

"Are you kidding? I've heard you moving things around in your room for the past hour. I figured you'd be down about now. What time are you leaving for Gramma Tessie's?"

"I told Henri I would meet her at the park at 10:30. We'll ride out together."

"Good. Then after breakfast, will you empty all the wastebaskets into a big trash bag and take it to the dumpster by the garage?"

"Sure, Mom. Anything else I can do for you?" *I can't believe I just asked that,* thought J.J.

Mom picked up on that right away. "Yes. The laundry needs to be done. The backyard needs to be mowed. The car needs a washing. Of course, there are always the windows." She smiled when she finished trying to think of some more things to add to the list.

"I don't have time for all that."

"You volunteered. Okay, just bring your laundry down and pile it by the washer. Then you might check your bicycle tires to be sure they are ready to go. Did you get that tire fixed?"

"Yes, thanks, Mom," he said as he took the stairs two at a time. In no time, he had his dirty clothes in front of the washer and was in the garage checking his bike. It was ready.

He parked the bike by the front porch and sat down in a chair to wait until 10:20. That was when he would leave. It would only take him a few minutes to ride to the park.

. . . .

Henri came downstairs at seven o'clock. She had gone to bed at ten o'clock the night before and had slept straight through. The nine hours of sleep had refreshed her.

I hope Gramma Tessie has some answers for us this morning, she thought. She walked into the kitchen and started getting things out for breakfast. She poured orange juice, selected a box of cereal from the cupboard, and filled a bowl. She poured some milk on the cereal and sat down at the table to eat.

"Hi, sis," said Joey as he entered the kitchen, startling Henri.

"What are you doing up so early?"

"I don't know. I woke up, so I came downstairs to watch TV. You're up early, too. Why?"

"I went to bed early, so I guess that's why I'm up early. Want some breakfast?"

"No thanks. I'll go watch TV for a while."

"Okay. I'll be in when I finish eating."

They watched TV for a while, and then Henri excused herself to go upstairs to her room to get ready.

"Where are you going?" Joey asked when she came back down.

"J.J. and I are riding out to Gramma's at 10:30."

"Is it a date?" he inquired. "Do you like J.J.?"

"No, it's not a date. Yes, I like J.J. We're friends and that's all. Gramma asked both of us to come out this morning. She must have something for us to help her do."

"Can I come along? I can ride that far."

"Another time. Gramma just asked for the two of us today. I'll ask her about bringing you along on the next swimming trip. Okay?"

"Sure. That'll be fun," he replied and went back to watching TV.

Henri walked into the kitchen to get a drink before leaving. Mom was sitting at the table reading the paper.

"Good morning, Henri. All set to go to Gramma's?"

"Yes. I was just leaving. I don't want to be late meeting J.J. at the park. See you around two o'clock or so."

"Okay. Ride safely."

"We will."

Henri arrived at the park first. There were only a couple of people there. One was walking on the far north side and was leaving the park. The other was a jogger who was leaving the park on the east side. Henri was entering the park on the southwest corner. She thought she was the only one there, but then she spotted a car ahead next to some large bushes.

Then she heard a scream and as she passed another large bush, she saw two men push a young mother down and grab her four- or five-year-old son by the arm.

"Mommy! Mommy!" he yelled. The jogger and the walker were too far away to hear. The poor little boy was frightened and was being lifted into the air as the men ran to their car. He continued to yell.

The mother screamed at the men. "Stop! Bring back my baby! Help! Police!" She got up but would not catch them in time.

"Ouch!" one of the men yelled. "The crazy kid bit me!"

"Shut up and throw him into the backseat!" the other man ordered.

"I can't! He's digging his fingers into my arm. Ouch! Stop that! All right, you asked for…"

Suddenly, they were frozen in place like statues.

"Here I am again in the middle of a dangerous situation because of this necklace. What do I do now?" Henri said out loud.

She looked around to see if there was anyone to help her. There at the far edge of the northwest side of the park was J.J., frozen in time on his bicycle.

"Great," she uttered. "This time I have some help."

She ran over to J.J. and touched his arm. He awakened, but the bicycle stayed frozen, motionless.

"What's going on?" he asked when he realized his bicycle had come to a stop. Then he saw Henri and understood.

"I need your help again. I had to stop time. Two men just kidnapped a little boy. They were carrying him to their car when I made time stand still."

"Let's get a closer look and see what we can do."

One man was reaching out holding the door open and trying to push the other man into the car. The second man had his right arm halfway around the boy who was in the air half in and half out of the car.

"Do you think we can get the boy without touching the man?" J.J. asked.

"I don't know. I sure don't want to wake up one of the men."

"Can we touch the car?"

"I think so. I touched our car when I got out last time and nothing happened. I'm not sure what happens to mechanical things during this time. They probably remain suspended until time starts again."

"Now what?" wondered J.J.

"Reach in the driver's side and turn the car off. Grab the keys," ordered Henri.

J.J. opened the car door. He turned off the engine and removed the keys from the ignition. Next, he opened the trunk. He found a tire iron he could use as a weapon. Then he threw the keys into a nearby bush.

"What's that for?" inquired a nervous Henri.

"It's a weapon. I might need it if one of these guys wakes up. I'm glad they are not very big."

"Now, let's see if we can get the little boy away from his abductor," Henri said. "Be very careful."

J.J. very carefully put his arms around the little boy. He pulled him out of the man's arm and held onto him. Then he walked a few steps away from the men.

The man was left holding nothing. He looked rather strange.

"What do we do now?"

Again, Henri had the answer. "Take the little boy to the far east side of the park. I'll come, too. We'll set him down near the bench way over there."

"Okay. But what about his mother?" J.J. wondered.

"We'll come back for her. I think we can carefully drag or carry her through the grass and sand. We'll leave her right next to the boy. When she wakes up, she can leave the park and get away."

J.J. carried the boy across the park, away from the would-be kidnappers. Henri walked along beside him. When they got back to the woman, J.J. said, "I want to use my small knife and let the air out of one of their tires before we move her."

"That's a good idea," Henri complimented. "It's nice to have someone to help with these situations."

"Yes. I know what you mean. I don't think we have to turn time back this time."

"No, we don't. One of us should go to the police station. It's three blocks north of here."

"I'll stay here," volunteered J.J. "First, let me get my bike from the other side of the park."

"Okay, but hurry."

J.J. ran across the park to his freestanding bicycle. He grabbed the handlebars, and the bike skidded towards him. "Oh, great! The wheels are frozen and won't turn." His voice showed his exasperation. "I'll have to carry it."

He lifted the bike and slowly carried it across the park. He put it down next to the little boy. Then he ran back to where Henri was standing.

"Okay," Henri stated. "Why don't you lift her by the arms, and I'll take her feet. Maybe we can carry her."

"Wait!" shouted J.J. "Don't touch her! You'll wake her up!"

"Oh, I forgot," an embarrassed Henri responded.

"I'll take her by the arms and drag her." Carefully, he took hold of the lady's wrists and slowly dragged her across the grass and through some sand. He put her down next to the boy. Henri walked along with them, carrying her bicycle.

"She's going to have some grass stains on her jeans, but at least she and her son are safe from those guys," J.J. stated with a little pride.

"I don't think she will mind," commented Henri.

"Now, you have to run to the police station. You can start up time again when you get there. Tell them what you saw and say that the lady and her son escaped. You can also tell them the kidnappers' car has a flat tire. Maybe they can get here in time to catch them."

"I'm not sure I want to get involved," Henri stated. "They will ask me to identify the abductors. I wouldn't feel safe if they knew who I was. The police will ask me lots of questions, and I might slip up and say something about stopping time. I sure don't want to do that."

The two kids stood there and looked at each other, trying to figure out what to do next.

23

"WHAT SHOULD WE DO?" HENRI ASKED.

"Could you do what you did during the convenience store robbery?"

"I could, but I wonder what they will think if another mysterious note appears at the police station."

J.J. smiled. "As long as you don't leave any fingerprints and your picture doesn't appear on their cameras, they'll never know it was you."

"I guess you're right."

"Don't start time until you get back here. Otherwise, you might get picked up on a camera between there and here."

"Okay," Henri replied. So off she ran to the police station. It only took her a few minutes to get there. Along the way, she passed people, dogs, cars, and bicyclists frozen in time.

Henri carefully backed into the door at the station. It looked the same as before, except for different officers inside. Three officers were clustered around one desk while another sat at the information desk. She pulled a tissue from her pocket and picked up a pen from an empty desk. She took another tissue out and used it to steady the small note tablet she had found. She wrote:

Go to Brightfield Park. Two men just tried to abduct a little boy from his mother. Their car has a flat tire. Hurry!

Henri decided to be doubly sure, so she wrote a second note saying exactly the same thing. She put one note on the desk in front of the man at the information desk. The other note she put on a desk farther back into the room where a solitary officer sat, staring off into space.

She wiped the pen using both tissues and placed it back on the desk where she found it. Then she used a tissue to pull the door open and stepped outside. She quickly ran back to the park. She stopped outside the park about thirty yards away from the mother and her son.

J.J. walked over to her carrying his bicycle. Luckily, they had good bikes that were very light. He had already carried Henri's bike over. Now, if time started again without her help, they could ride away.

"Let's start riding away as soon as you start time," J.J. suggested. "We can look back and see what's happening. When the two men see their flat tire and can't find their keys, they'll leave the mother and her son alone."

"The police will probably be here in a few minutes. We need to be out of sight by then. What did you do with the tire iron?"

"I think I left it on the ground once I got the kid free."

"Run back and get it. I'll need to wipe off your fingerprints. Then I can throw it under a bush."

J.J. retrieved the tire iron. Henri used her tissues to hold it and wipe it clean. Carrying it with tissue-covered fingers, she placed it under a large bushy plant across the street from the park.

"Okay, let's go. We don't have much time left."

Before Henri could reach for the necklace, time started again. They quickly got on their bicycles and started to ride away.

They heard a scream from behind them. "Help! Help! Those two men tried to take my son! Help! Police!" She picked her son up and started to hurry away from the men.

J.J. and Henri turned a corner and did not see what happened next. They had safely made it out of the situation.

Two men came into the park jogging in the mother's direction. She yelled at them, "Call 9-1-1! Those two men tried to kidnap my son!"

One of the men pulled out a cell phone and made the call. The other stepped toward the lady and said, "It's all right, ma'am. We're off-duty police officers." He showed her his credentials.

Before they could approach the two men, the sound of sirens could be heard getting louder as the cars neared the park. Three police cars pulled up next to the kidnappers' car and two officers got out of each car. The two kidnappers were quickly apprehended.

The police officers noticed an elderly couple sitting on a bench under a tree about fifty yards away. They were facing this way. After talking with them, the officers learned they had seen the attempted kidnapping and could confirm the mother's accusations.

"Should we have stayed to see what happened?" asked J.J.

"No. I think it's better if we stay invisible. Let's not take any chances. We'll tell Gramma Tessie about this and see what she thinks. Everything should be okay because we heard the police sirens. I bet they got there in time to arrest those two guys."

"I have lots of questions for Gramma Tessie," J.J. said.

"Me, too," added Henri.

They continued on their way and got to Gramma Tessie's house at eleven o'clock. She was loading something into her SUV.

"Hi, kids. How was the ride?"

"Great," replied Henri.

"We had some excitement at the park," continued J.J. "You'll never believe what happened."

"Don't be so sure. You can tell me about it while I drive. Put your bikes in the garage. I'll shut the door from inside the Tahoe. Then we'll be on our way."

"Where are we going, Gramma?" inquired Henri.

"You'll find out when we get there. It will take us about a half hour or so. You'll recognize the place when you see it."

"Why the secrecy, Gramma?"

"It's necessary. I'll explain when we get there. Just sit tight and enjoy the ride."

Gramma pushed several buttons on her console before they started. A low hum could be heard from somewhere above them. She drove north two miles and then turned west. She drove six or seven more miles before turning south.

"What's that hum, Gramma?" Henri asked.

"It's a special device I had installed that helps the GPS. I'll turn on the radio so you won't hear the hum."

"Gramma, we have something to tell you," started Henri. "Something happened yesterday. I broke one of the rules you gave me regarding the necklace."

"Don't worry, dear. Everything happens for a reason. Tell me about it."

"We almost had an accident. I used the necklace to stop time just before a truck ran into an old man and his dog. Then when I tried to get out of the car, I accidentally touched J.J. He woke up and learned about my power."

Henri now had tears in her eyes. Her voice cracked when she tried to continue. "I…I'm sorry, Gramma. I didn't mean to tell J.J. about my necklace. And then when we tried to save the man, his dog ended up being killed anyway. I really messed up," she sobbed. "J.J. told me about his power to turn time back one hour because he had to use it to help save the man. I'm so sorry," she said as the tears flowed down her cheeks.

"Nonsense, my dear. You did very well. You saved the man, didn't you? You and J.J. learned about each other's power. Now, you have someone to talk to. So does J.J."

"How come you don't seem surprised to hear about our powers, Gramma Tessie?" asked a bewildered J.J.

"Oh, I've known for a long time. That's what this meeting is about. It's the next step. If you hadn't already learned about each other's power, you would have been told today."

"So, it's okay that I shared my secret with J.J.?" questioned Henri.

"Yes. And it's also okay that he shared with you."

After four miles of driving south, Gramma Tessie turned east onto Birch Bark Road. "Oh, look! We're almost there."

"Gramma Tessie, this is the road where Grams' farm is located. Is that where we're going?" asked J.J.

"Yes, it is. She's expecting us. Don't ask any questions. We'll both have some answers for you once we get there."

"You sure took the long way to get to Grams' farm," J.J. added.

"I wanted to be sure we were not followed. We are about to have a very important meeting."

And then they arrived. Once the Tahoe was parked in the circle drive, they made their way into the house through the side door. Grams was waiting in the living room.

"Come in. Did you have a good trip out here?" she asked with a big smile.

"Did you see us come in from the west? We must have driven thirteen or fourteen miles to get here," replied J.J. "Why did we need to be sure no one followed us?"

"You will know in just a few more minutes. However, when we start to answer some of your questions, our answers will leave you with even more questions."

Grams got up and locked the door through which they had entered. "Follow me, please." She led the way down the short hallway into the first bedroom. Gramma Tessie closed the door behind them. Then Grams opened the closet door. The closet was not as deep as a normal closet, but there was still room to hang clothes.

Next, Grams spread a few of the clothes off to the side. She reached up toward the ceiling and pressed a button. Slowly, the shoe rack swung out from the wall. Grams pushed a button on the back of the shoe rack and part of the wall slid away, revealing a hidden room. An eerie glow was coming from inside.

"Hello," said a familiar voice, "come in and sit down. We have a lot to talk about."

The kids were both shocked to see who was motioning them into the dimly lit room.

24

IT HAD BEEN A LONG TRIP FROM SAROS BACK TO EARTH. HE felt like he was home again. Dr. M felt an allegiance to both worlds.

Before going to bed, he set the sophisticated alarm system he had installed on his house. He had anticipated trouble someday with the military from Saros coming to Earth. He tried to protect himself the best he could.

He awoke at eight o'clock the next morning. *I have to handle the spy situation. But first, there is something even more important that needs to be done,* he thought to himself.

"I think I'll go into town and see if the school is open. I'll be working with seventh and eighth grades this year. I need to pick up some things at the school to make preparations," he said out loud. This would give the Saronians something to think about when they listened to the recordings.

He ate a leisurely breakfast and then entered the side door of the attached garage through the kitchen. He reset the alarm just before he left the house.

Once in the garage, he got into his SUV and started it. Then, after opening the garage door, he drove out, closing the door behind him.

It was only ten o'clock, so he drove through town and stopped at the middle school. It was locked, so he drove to the district office that was open all summer.

He went into the personnel office and was warmly greeted by the receptionist. She pushed a button and announced his arrival. "Dr. Stone will see you right away," she announced. "Go right back to his office."

"Thank you," he replied.

Dr. Stone, the assistant superintendent of personnel, was a friend of Dr. M. They greeted each other and then talked about ten minutes. Dr. Stone handed Dr. M a set of keys to the middle school's outside doors as well as to his new office. He also gave him the alarm code written on a piece of paper.

"Memorize this and shred the paper," Dr. Stone advised. "I think you will find the middle school kids an interesting mix."

"I'm sure I will. Hopefully, I can help them get the classes they need, plus I can help them with any problems that come up."

"I'm sure you can. This counseling position is new this year. We think the middle school kids need someone they can talk to. I think you are the perfect person for this job."

"I'll do my best," concluded Dr. M as he rose and shook Dr. Stone's hand. "See you when school starts."

"Enjoy the rest of your summer," replied Dr. Stone. He turned to answer his telephone that had begun to ring.

Dr. M's attention was drawn to a mother and her teenage son walking toward him as he was leaving the district office. He noticed a slight glow around the teenager. He decided to investigate.

"Hi," he said as they met. "My name is Dr. Emory. The kids call me Dr. M. I'm the seventh and eighth grade counselor at the middle school."

"Hi," the lady replied. "I'm Torah Gotto. This is my son, Hunter. He'll be in tenth grade this year."

"Hello, Hunter," Dr. M said. "I hope your sophomore year is a good one."

"It won't be. This is the third school I've attended in the past three years. Next year, I'll probably be someplace else."

"I'm sorry to hear that. Is there anything I can do to help? Do you know anyone in Millville?"

"I don't know anyone, and I don't want to know anyone! The sooner we get out of this dumpy little town, the better!"

"I'm sorry, Dr. Emory," Mrs. Gotto sighed. "Hunter doesn't do well in school. All he cares about is running. He's also not very polite. I guess that's why he doesn't make friends easily."

"Mom! I don't need friends. Why are you telling a stranger all about me? He doesn't care about me."

"That's where you are wrong, Hunter," Dr. M replied. "I care about all the students in the Millville schools. In fact, I've taught many of them while teaching sixth grade the past few years."

"You can't fool me," Hunter responded. "What's your angle?"

"No angle. Stop by my office after school starts. I'd love to hear about your plans for your future. Perhaps I can help."

"Nobody can help me. I'm a loner. Come on, Mom. Let's get this over with."

"I'm sorry, Dr. Emory. We need to get inside and register Hunter."

"We have very good cross-country and track teams. We took first place last year in the Alamo County Classic Meet. There were several state champions in the high school. You could join one of the teams."

"That'll be the day. I've run faster every year for the past three years. I can run circles around anybody in this little town. There's no challenge in that."

"Do you know anyone in town, Mrs. Gotto?" Dr. M asked, smiling at her.

"Yes. My aunt lives on a lake near here," she replied.

"What's her name?" Dr. M inquired.

"Tessie Matthews," was her reply. "My parents moved away from here many years ago. We've not kept in touch with Tessie. She will be very surprised to see us."

"She doesn't know you're here in Millville?" Dr. M asked.

"No," Mrs. Gotto said. "We arrived in town yesterday. We're staying at the motel until I can rent us an apartment. I'll start work at the manufacturing plant next week."

"Welcome to Millville," Dr. M replied. "Here's my card. Call me if you need help in any way."

"Thank you," she said.

"Hope you change your mind, Hunter. Cross-country practice starts the week before Labor Day."

"Don't hold your breath," Hunter replied. "I might come once just to see how slow the runners in this dinky little town are."

Dr. M turned and walked toward his car. Mrs. Gotto and Hunter went into the office to register for fall classes.

So this is Tessie's niece, he thought. *I've never seen a Saronian aura as bright as Hunter's. I wonder if the yellow sun is responsible.*

Dr. M left the district office and drove south out of town. After six miles, he pushed several buttons on his dash. A low hum could be heard coming from his ceiling.

He turned west and drove a few miles before turning north. One more turn and he was heading east. He had driven in all four directions to be sure no one had followed him.

He arrived at his destination at 10:45. He parked next to Grams' car outside the garage. He walked up to the house where a very nice lady greeted him. She led him inside.

"So it's time to reveal everything?" she asked.

"Yes, it is. Let's hope it goes well. Are they on their way?"

"They are. I just spoke with their driver, and she said she would get them here shortly after eleven o'clock."

"Well, then, I'll go to the control room and prepare things for them."

"I'm so glad you were able to get back in time for this meeting, Dr. M," Grams explained. "Tessie and I were a little nervous about handling it without you."

"You would have done just fine. But I am glad to be back," he replied. He went through the closet and into the secret room and pressed a button. Lights came on and dimly lit the room. Two computer screens lit up, and two computer keyboards began to glow. Two TV screens unrolled out of the ceiling. He closed the door to the room, and he was alone.

Everything was ready. There were five chairs and Dr. M sat down in one to wait.

It was about forty-five minutes later when the door reopened and four people stood staring into the small room.

Dr. M rose and said, "Hello, come in and sit down. We have a lot to talk about."

Henri and J.J. were speechless. Grams gave them each a little push. The four of them entered the crowded room.

"Please sit down," Dr. M offered.

Grams reached over and pushed a button. The door in the wall noiselessly closed.

Finally, J.J. found his voice. "What are you doing here, Dr. M? Why are we here? Grams, what's this all about?"

"I'm as baffled as J.J.," remarked Henri. "What is this room? Why are there computers and TV screens showing several Earth continents?"

"We will explain everything in the next several minutes. This meeting is about your necklace and his bracelet. You are about to learn some extraordinary things. Some of them may scare you, but we're here to help you."

"Yes, we are," Gramma Tessie reassured them. Her calm, soothing voice had the desired effect. J.J. and Henri gradually calmed and relaxed a little.

"Here, have a drink of water," suggested Grams. She handed both kids a bottle of water.

"Tell me what you know about each other's powers," Dr. M said, looking at J.J.

"Well, I know about Henri's necklace and her power to stop time for one hour. And I can see her necklace when no one else can. We worked together to save a man yesterday, but we were not able to save his little dog. Just before coming here, we rescued a small boy who was about to be kidnapped."

"And I know about J.J.'s power to turn back time an hour. We talked for a while last night at a park so no one could overhear us," added Henri.

"It's good that you know about each other. It will build camaraderie. You must learn to work together," continued

Dr. M. "It sounds like you have already done that quite successfully."

"There's a lot more to this than you realize," Grams stated. "We are about to tell you a seemingly unbelievable story. Having experienced your special abilities should help you understand what we're going to say."

Dr. M spoke next. "We will tell you everything we know but will save the most extraordinary part for last. That will be the hardest to understand. When we finish, we will leave the two of you in here to talk about everything. Are you ready?"

"I guess so," replied Henri.

"Go ahead," added J.J.

Dr. M started. "The powers that you have come from the special stones you are wearing. Those stones have now blended with your bodies. That's why no one can see them. It's for your protection. You can see each other's stone because the one you wear gives you that ability.

"I have brought with me two more stones. There is another boy and another girl who will receive them. The four of you will become a team, although you will often work in pairs."

"What will we be doing?" inquired Henri.

"Just what you have been doing. You will learn to use your powers in many circumstances. You will learn to coordinate your abilities for the good of everyone.

"Now, there is something a lot bigger going on. This will be hard to believe. Hopefully, seeing time stand still and then seeing time back up an hour will allow your minds to grasp the bigger picture."

"Are you with us so far?" asked Grams.

"I don't know what to think," J.J. replied. "This is beyond belief."

"Me, too," Henri added. "I'm shocked. I don't know what to say."

"That's understandable," soothed Dr. M.

"This has been planned for a long time," added Gramma Tessie. "Okay, Dr. M, give them the rest of the facts."

"The stones you are wearing come from a planet 1.4 light-years away from Earth. They are special because of where they are from, and they are being made more powerful by your yellow sun. They come from a dying planet revolving around a red sun.

"The planet is called Saros. Much of the water on Saros has been contaminated. There are only twenty-five or so years left for the people living there before the water runs out. Then everyone will die.

"Several military men, as well as some civilians, have learned about Earth and its abundant water supply. They want to invade and conquer Earth. This presents a problem for them because Earth's yellow sun is poisonous to Saronians. They can only stay here two months. They will die if they do not return to Saros for special treatment."

"I don't think I can believe this," J.J. commented. "We don't have interplanetary space travel. There's no other life in our solar system. How can we believe there's life on another planet that wants to conquer Earth?"

"J.J., I've been reading a little about the universe," Henri said. "You know how unbelievably large it is. We can't comprehend its size. Just our own Milky Way Galaxy is approximately 100,000 light-years across. A light-year is the distance light travels in a vacuum in a year at a speed of 186,000 miles per second. To get that in miles per hour, we would have to multiply 186,000 by 60 and then by 60 again." Henri picked up a pencil and did some quick multiplying on a piece of paper lying on the desk. "That would be 670,000,000 miles per hour.

"Now, compare that to Voyager I that was launched from Earth in 1977. In thirty-five years, it has traveled sixteen light hours from Earth. At its speed of 36,000 miles per hour, it will take 17,500 years to reach one light-year's distance from Earth!

"One light-year equals about six trillion miles. Saros is 1.4 light-years away from Earth. It is still in our galaxy." She did some more calculations and then concluded, "That makes it 8.4 trillion miles away."

Dr. M continued, "We are able to travel here because of a wormhole that allows a 'shortcut' as we might call it. There are probably more wormholes out there waiting to be discovered. They are what makes traveling long distances possible for us."

"The Andromeda Galaxy is nearly 2.5 megalight-years away from Earth," Henri continued. "A megalight-year is

1,000,000 light-years. When we multiply, we get 2.5 million light years or 15,000,000,000,000,000,000 miles."

"These numbers even I cannot understand," Dr. M stated. "We know there are millions of galaxies in the universe. Doesn't it seem reasonable that there could be life out there somewhere?"

"Wow! That was a lot of information, Henri. How do you know so much about the universe?" J.J. asked.

"Some of this material we covered in class last year. The rest I picked up in my reading," she replied.

"I still don't think I can believe this," J.J. said.

"J.J.," Henri said, "you're a *Star Trek* fan. Look at all the different kinds of life those people discovered."

"That's make-believe. This is real life, Henri," he replied.

"We thought you might feel this way. We will show you some proof if you are ready to see it," suggested Dr. M.

"Okay," a hesitant J.J. responded. "What kind of proof are you talking about? Are you going to show us an alien?"

"Would you believe us if we showed you one?" asked Gramma Tessie.

"How about if we showed you three aliens?" suggested Grams.

"No way!" said J.J. "Are you saying that you three are aliens?"

"Grams and I are your real grandmothers. Our grandfathers were among the first Saronians to come to Earth peacefully and secretly. They nearly all died because of Earth's yellow sun. However, your grandfathers developed a pulse machine that purified their blood and modified their cellular structure that kept them alive."

Grams continued the story. "I was born two years after we arrived here. My father's friend and his wife had a son around the same time. We grew up, fell in love, and were married. Your father was our only child, J.J."

"My story is similar," Gramma Tessie added. "Two of the other couples each had a child. Somehow, their children fell in love and were married. Your father, Henri, was their only child. None of them were related to each other.

"The interesting part of the story started when your two fathers fell in love with Earth women. Permission from Saros was granted for their marriages. Both of your mothers were made aware of where their spouse's families had come from. That made no difference to them."

"So, you can see that both of you can trace your ancestry through your fathers back to Saros," explained Dr. M. "You are the first of four to be born of Earth women. That may be why you have been chosen by the Saros stones."

"How can we believe this?" J.J. asked incredulously. "This is impossible!"

"Is stopping time impossible? Is turning time back, reliving it, and changing it impossible? And yet you have seen it yourselves," Dr. M said. "It's time. I will be first. I will show you proof that you cannot argue with. Are you ready?"

"I think so," J.J. very slowly replied.

"I'm scared," Henri said. Again, she had tears running down her cheeks. "Will everything be okay, Gramma?"

"Yes, dear," comforted Gramma Tessie as she hugged Henri. "Everything will be fine. Nothing will change. You will just have a lot of information to process. You are two very important people. The stones you wear and the powers you are developing are a part of a prophecy made on Saros many generations ago."

Wiping the tears from her cheeks, Henri said, "All right. Go ahead."

Dr. M spoke next. "We are going to allow our features to change into their normal configuration. My features will change more dramatically because I was born on Saros. We will still be the same people. Your grandmothers will still love you. We are going to have to work together and fight together to save Earth from a possible invasion by a superior force, and also try to find a way to save the people of Saros."

Slowly, all three adults changed. Their ears grew slightly larger. Their heads became more elongated up and down. Their skin turned a bronze color. A slight glow emanated from Dr. M's body. His eyes narrowed a little and their color changed to a golden tan with yellow flecks all through them. His nose pulled back into his face and became flatter. The grandmothers' skin did not glow and their eyes did not change color.

J.J. and Henri's eyes got larger. Their mouths opened as they stared, but no words came out.

Grams reached out and pushed a red button next to the door. Noiselessly, the door slid into the wall, creating the opening through which they had entered. The three adults left without saying another word, and the wall slid back into place, leaving J.J. and Henri to discuss what they had learned.

25

J.J. AND HENRI SAT, STARING AT EACH OTHER. FINALLY, J.J. broke the silence.

"I don't know what to say," he muttered. "How can this possibly be true? And if it is, what do we do next?"

"At least, we're not in this alone. We have three adults who care about us. They'll help us adjust to the use of our new powers. And soon we'll have two more kids our age to work with and confide in. That won't be so bad."

"No, I guess not. But what are we supposed to do with these new powers? I get scared when I turn time back and then try to change a catastrophe into something good."

"I know," continued Henri. "I feel the same way when I stop time and try to keep something bad from happening. I'm afraid I'll make a mistake and make things worse."

"Maybe with Dr. M's help, we'll get more comfortable using our powers. It seemed a lot easier working with you when we saved the boy from the kidnappers."

"Yes, it was easier working with you than all by myself. I think I could get used to that."

It was quiet for a few minutes while they each thought.

"J.J.," Henri finally said, "let's ask about our fathers. I'll bet they're connected to this somehow."

"Good idea. Is there anything else we should ask?"

"Yes. When will the other two join us? How do we fit into the lack of water on Saros and the invasion plans?"

"Okay then. Let's go out and talk with them."

Henry rapped on the door, but no one responded. She rapped again, this time much louder. "Perhaps this is a sound proof room," she said. She turned to J.J. and asked, "Should we push the red button and open the door?"

"Do we have a choice?" J.J. asked right back.

"No, I guess not. But you push the button. I'm keeping my hands around my necklace in case there's trouble out there. I'm getting a premonition that something is wrong."

"Good idea. I'm feeling it, too." J.J. pushed the button and the doorway appeared. No one was there. Cautiously, they crept through the closet and peered into the bedroom.

It was quite dark in there as Grams kept the blinds pulled down and the curtains pulled together.

"There's no one here," gasped J.J. "Dr. M? Grams? Gramma Tessie? Are you out there?" he asked in a whispery voice.

When no answer came, they both slowly and quietly stepped from the closet. The bedroom was empty. Now, they were both getting edgy.

"Let's peek into the living room," whispered Henri.

"Okay," he replied. He was reluctant to take the first step.

So Henri went first. As she peeked around the corner from the short hallway into the living room, a stunning sight greeted her eyes.

There was Grams tied to a chair with a gag in her mouth. Gramma Tessie was gagged and tied to another chair in the corner. Dr. M was face down on the floor with a pool of blood slowly seeping out from under him. Both grandmothers' eyes moved from the kids across the room to where six men with strange weapons stood.

Henri screamed and placed her thumbs into the necklace she held tightly in her hands. The last thing she heard was a deep voice yelling, "Shut up, you stupid kid!"

Then time stood still.

Quickly, Henri touched J.J. on the shoulder and awakened him.

"What happened here?" she asked.

"I don't know, but let's check Dr. M. I hope he's still alive."

"He must be! He has to be!" Henri shouted. "Dr. M! Wake up!" She carefully touched his shoulder. He moaned and slowly rolled over. There was a big lump on his head and a little blood oozed from it. He had a cut on his arm, and that was where all the blood on the floor was coming from.

They helped him sit up. Henri ran to the bathroom and returned with a towel. She wrapped it tightly around his arm. He was quite dazed from the blow to his head.

"What happened?" the kids chorused together.

"We decided to wait here in the living room while you two talked," Dr. M responded slowly. "We had been talking for ten minutes or so when six soldiers from Saros broke down the side door and attacked us. One of them hit me on the head with his rifle. I must have fallen over the coffee table and broken the glass. They must have tied Grams and Tessie up while I was unconscious. Let's wake them up and find out what happened."

Henri walked over and undid the gag from Gramma Tessie. J.J. did the same for Grams. Then Henri touched each of them.

Henri and J.J. were still untying them when they both started talking at the same time.

"One at a time," Dr. M commanded.

"Go ahead, Grams. You tell it," Gramma Tessie suggested.

"After they knocked you out, they started asking us questions. They wanted to know where the two kids were who came in with Tessie. They demanded to know why we were all here. They yelled at Tessie and wanted to know why she had mentioned Saros stones to Henri several months ago. They also wanted to know who we were and how we knew you, Dr. M."

"Was that all?" Dr. M questioned. "Did they know you were Saronians?"

"They did not know we were from Saros, but they asked again about the kids. They got mad when I told them I had dropped them off in Davisburg. That's when they tied us up and gagged us. They threatened to torture us. Then Henri and J.J. came into the room and Henri screamed."

"How were you able to stop time before they grabbed you?" Dr. M asked.

"We both felt something was wrong," Henri answered. "So I held my necklace in my hands as we peeked out from the hallway."

"That was good thinking. Lucky for all of us you were able to stop time before they got to you," Dr. M complimented. "Now, we have to decide how to handle this."

"How did they know we were here? Our jamming devices should have prevented their tracking us," Tessie stated.

"They might have put a locator on one of our cars. Once we arrived and turned off the jammer, they could have received the signal and followed it here," Dr. M explained.

"Where did these soldiers come from? I didn't think soldiers were being sent so soon," Grams wanted to know.

"They must have moved up the timetable. We have underestimated them. We cannot let that happen again. Perhaps those three spies were not as incompetent as I thought," Dr. M continued. "Now, we have to make a plan."

"Yes," J.J. chimed in. "I can turn time back one hour, but will that be before or after they arrived here?"

"Let's hope it's before. We have some work to do before you turn time back. Grams, I assume you are packed and ready to leave."

"Yes. I have two suitcases ready to take with me at a moment's notice."

"Well, that moment has arrived," Dr. M added in a determined voice. "This has been a wonderful farm, and I hate to see it destroyed."

"We have no choice if they have discovered its location," Grams countered. "It has served its purpose."

"When time starts up again, we all need to know what we are going to do," Dr. M stated. "It has been about five minutes since you stopped time, Henri. It was 12:00 when we came out here and were surprised by these men. It is now 12:15. We talked with you in the control room for about ten minutes, and then you two talked together for another ten minutes. What we don't know is how long they were outside waiting before they came inside and attacked us. We'll hope they had just arrived when they broke down the door and captured us. That should mean we will have somewhere around twenty minutes from when you start time until the soldiers arrive."

"What do you want us to do?" asked Henri.

"When time turns back, Tessie and you two kids will be almost here. Continue until you get here but drive a little faster. Once you arrive, park your car up close to the garage next to my car. Get into Grams' car where she will be waiting. We will all leave in her car. We will drive out the back way using the tractor road behind the barn that leads to the orchard.

"We will stop on the far side of the orchard. I will come back through the cornfield with my binoculars and watch what happens. We need to know if the soldiers escape or not.

"When I return to the car, we will drive around through Hamilton and then back to Millville."

"What do you mean 'if the soldiers escape or not'?" Henri asked tentatively.

"This is war, Henri," Dr. M responded. "You saw how those soldiers treated us. They would have killed me and tortured the ladies to get the information they wanted. They might have killed all of us. This is just the beginning. There will be casualties. I hope that with the help of your new powers, and those of the other two soon to join us, the casualties will be minimal."

"This is happening too fast," J.J. said. "I can't keep up."

"You will learn. Hopefully, you will have time to understand and use the full extent of your powers. The fate of Earth, as well as Saros, hangs in the balance."

"What will happen to the farm, Dr. M?" Henri asked.

"It has been rigged with a special disintegration bomb I brought from Saros several years ago. I will remotely detonate it from the field right behind the barn. It is imperative that the soldiers either be inside the house or very close to it."

"What will the bomb do?" J.J. wanted to know.

"It will disintegrate everything within fifty yards of it. There will be nothing left of the house or the cars. The barn will be the only building left standing. Where the house is, there will only be the hole where the basement is. No trace of the house or the cars will be left behind for anyone to examine.

"I will leave the radio on in the control room so they will hear it when they enter the house. Once they find the control room, the leader will want to examine it. This will seem like a very big discovery for them.

"Once the house and cars are gone, I'll return to Grams' car, and we'll get out of here. I have a special device hidden in my garage that will disclose the whereabouts of any Saronian within 1,000 miles. We also have a device that will work from a ship in orbit. We must determine how many military people are here."

"This has suddenly become very serious and dangerous business," Grams exclaimed.

"Yes, it has," Tessie responded. "You can move into my house for a while until we decide what to do next."

"Thank you," Grams replied.

"Are we in any danger?" Henri asked.

"I'm not sure," Dr. M answered. "We'll know more once we determine how many Saronians are in the area. I suspect you are safe for now. Even if they suspect you of something, there is no evidence that either of you represents a threat to them. I'm the one they are after."

"Will you go into hiding?" Gramma Tessie inquired.

"No, not right away. We need more information first. Then I'll decide what to do. We must get the last two Saros stones to the others who will help us.

"I think we are ready to start time up again as soon as the five of us get outside the house and away from these men. Five seconds after Henri starts time, J.J., you turn time back. We'll meet right back here and put our plan into action."

Dr. M went into the control room and returned with a small weapon. Then they all went outside and hid on the west side of the house out of sight of the soldier guarding the cars.

Dr. M motioned to Henri. She started time up again. Five seconds later, J.J. turned time back one hour…

....

Just like that J.J., Henri, and Gramma Tessie were back in the car heading for Grams' farmhouse. However, this time, the kids knew what to expect.

"This is still strange, reliving things a second time. It's scary knowing that something bad could happen to us," Henri said.

"Things will work just fine," Gramma Tessie encouraged. "Dr. M has a lot of experience dealing with situations like this. He also has a few tricks up his sleeve. You'll see."

"I sure hope so," J.J. replied not so confidently.

"I'm driving a little faster than before. We'll be there in five minutes. That will put us ten minutes earlier than last time."

Sure enough, they arrived at Grams' farm at 11:20. Grams was in the car by the garage, waiting. They parked and were out of their car and in Grams' car in about fifteen seconds. Dr. M came out the side door of the garage and got into their car about fifteen minutes later.

"You made good time, Tessie," Dr. M complimented. "I think everything is ready."

"Thank you," Tessie replied. "Now, let's get out of here!"

Grams was already backing the car up as Tessie was speaking. She drove straight toward the barn, made a left behind the old out building, and followed a path around behind the barn. She followed the tractor path between the barn and the cornfield behind it. Then she drove along the path into the cornfield next to the barn. Now, they were out of sight from the house.

"Stop here, Grams," Dr. M ordered. "We have about thirty-five minutes to wait. I'll meet you on the far side of the orchard."

"Please be careful," Henri sobbed.

"Don't worry. I'll be back soon, and we can start to make some serious plans for your future, our future. Keep the car running and the anti-tracking jammer turned on. Stay in the car with the doors locked."

Dr. M got out of the car and carefully made his way through the cornfield. He had to duck a little to keep his head lower than the corn stalks.

This is a good crop of corn, he thought. *It's almost as tall as I am.*

He was able to get past the barn and still stay in the cornfield. He could see the driveway, the yard, and the house. He was fifteen feet or so from the edge of the field and was well hidden. The house was about fifty yards away. He could not set off the bomb from here. He was too close.

He checked his watch. It was 11:40, thirty minutes earlier than when the soldiers attacked before. He'd stay hidden and watch for them. The detonator was in his right hand, and he looked at it. It was ready.

While Dr. M was getting into position behind the barn, Grams drove through the orchard. J.J. had to get out and walk in front of the car to move the branches that had fallen onto the old path. This was the route the farmer used to take between fields. Now, the modern equipment was too large to fit the narrow path.

When they arrived at the far end of the orchard, Grams turned the car south and stopped. The path ahead looked clear, and it was only about a quarter of a mile to the main road.

J.J. got back inside the car, and they waited for Dr. M to return. There was nothing more any of them could do. Once time was turned back, J.J. and Henri could not alter it again until the full hour had passed.

No one could think of anything to say. So much had happened in the past hour that they were all somewhat distraught. So they waited in silence.

26

"IS THERE A SIGNAL YET?" DEMANDED CAPTAIN MONTEFORD.

"No, sir," replied Sergeant Lowell. "She must still be driving. There must be something blocking the signal while the car is turned on."

"I told you we should have followed her," Private Thompson said.

"We couldn't take the chance that she would see us," Captain Monteford sternly replied. "There is not much traffic on these old country roads. If she is up to something, she will be careful not to be followed."

"I have something," interrupted Sergeant Lowell. "There is a blip on the screen five miles southwest of Millville. That must be her destination."

"We must go quickly," Captain Monteford commanded. "It will only take us ten minutes to get there."

The six soldiers got into two cars and headed out of Millville. They had been waiting in the big IGA grocery store parking lot.

"What happens when we get there?" asked Private Thompson.

"We capture them and force them to tell us what they are planning," Captain Monteford replied. "Dr. M will talk if we threaten to harm the kids or the old women."

"What if they will not talk?" Sergeant Lowell questioned.

"They are way out in the country," Captain Monteford replied. "We will torture them until they tell us what we want to know. It will not be a great loss if they die in the process. Then we will not have to worry about Dr. M's interference anymore."

They followed the roads leading to the signal from their tracking device. Finally, they approached the farmhouse on Birch Bark Road.

"There is the car parked by the garage," Sergeant Lowell observed. "And that is Dr. M's car right next to it. This could not be better."

"Check your weapons, men," Captain Monteford ordered. "Set them to immobilize and not to kill. Do not fire unless I order it." He radioed the men in the car behind them with the same instructions.

. . . .

A little while later, Dr. M saw two cars approaching. They pulled into the driveway and parked right behind the two cars already there.

This will keep them from driving away, thought Captain Monteford.

Quickly, the six men piled out of the cars. "You stay here and guard the cars, Private Thompson. Make sure no one escapes this way. We will go in the door on the other side of the house."

"Yes, sir," he replied.

Captain Monteford led the way around to the outside door and found it unlocked. However, the inside door was locked.

"Break it down!" he ordered.

Two soldiers kicked the door at the same time. It was knocked back into the house.

"Hands up! Nobody move! You are our prisoners!" shouted Captain Monteford.

There was no one there. Then they heard a voice coming from farther inside the house.

"You stand guard here, Private Monroe. Watch those stairs we passed that lead to the basement. The rest of you follow me."

With his gun pointed in front of him, Captain Monteford led the soldiers into the living room.

"It is coming from that hallway. Sergeant Lowell, take Mayfield and investigate," Captain Monteford ordered.

"Yes, sir. Mayfield, follow me."

A minute later they returned. "The voice is coming from a room hidden behind a closet in the bedroom. The room is filled with sophisticated electronic equipment. There is a TV screen broadcasting the news. You better have a look at it, sir."

"I think we have found their communications center. Destroying this will set them back a lot," Captain Monteford stated after inspecting the small room.

"But where are the people?" asked Sergeant Lowell.

"I do not know," replied Captain Monteford. "Search the rest of the house. I will try to get some information from the computer in there. Then we will destroy everything here."

One soldier checked the downstairs rooms while one went upstairs.

Captain Monteford went back to the control room, sat down, and started typing on the keyboard, trying to gain access to the files within.

Outside in the cornfield, Dr. M had watched as one soldier was stationed near the car and the other five entered the house. He looked down at his watch. Five minutes after they entered the house, he depressed the timer button on his remote. It was set for three minutes. He watched the first minute pass on the timer. Then he turned away and started back toward the orchard. When he was halfway there, he checked the timer. There were twenty seconds left. He lay down on the ground facing away from the house. He covered his head with his hands and waited.

Twenty seconds later, he saw a bright flash even though his eyes were shut. Then he heard a loud boom followed by the rush of wind. The corn was bent as the powerful blast of air blew past.

Then things were still again.

Dr. M peeked above the tops of the corn, and he could not see the farmhouse. He crept back past the barn and came to the spot from which he had watched the soldiers arrive.

The house, the cars, and both outbuildings were gone! The hole for the basement was all that remained. All the trees around the house were disintegrated.

"Looks like we win this round," Dr. M solemnly commented. "But I bet it'll get rougher from now on."

He stood up and ran through the fields to the waiting car. He had been gone 45 minutes.

"We saw the flash and heard the boom. And then there was a blast of air that shook the car. Did it work? Are we safe?" asked J.J.

"Yes," replied Dr. M. "The house, the cars, and all the soldiers are gone. No one will know they were here."

"Then let's get out of here!" Grams exclaimed. "We need to get to Tessie's house and debrief. What do we do about the lost cars?"

"We'll work that out," Dr. M said. "Are you kids okay? You've had to endure a lot today. I'm proud of the way you've handled yourselves!"

"I'm okay," Henri replied. "I don't think this has all soaked in yet."

"I agree," J.J. added. "Let's get back to Gramma Tessie's house and talk about everything that's happened. Henri and I have some questions to ask."

There was silence as Grams drove them back to Tessie's house. Everyone was thinking about the past hour and wondering what the future held.

27

DALE AND HAROLD WERE VERY EXCITED. THEY WERE finally headed home! Their ship had landed on Triton, and they were beginning their work.

"Do you think we can reclaim the water here?" Dale asked.

"I don't know. We'll need to bring some samples into the ship's laboratory and study them. Let's suit up and get outside."

Twenty minutes later, the two scientists were standing on the rugged landscape of Triton. They spent an hour collecting samples and then returned to the ship.

After two hours of work, they discussed their findings. "The nitrogen, ammonia, and methane are inseparable," an exasperated Dale finally said. "I had hoped this would work."

"I know," added Harold. "What about the 'ice' in the rings orbiting the planet?"

"I don't think there is enough volume there to sustain an entire planet, and we'll probably find similar compounds as those here on the surface. I think 'ice' is a poor word choice. I assume it's because these compounds solidify at cold temperatures. There's probably no water in them at all."

"This is a fine situation. At least, we helped with the conservation efforts on Saros. That will keep them going for a couple of decades while they look for a permanent solution."

"I think relocation is the only answer," Harold concluded. "I just don't want it to be to Earth."

"I agree. There must be a planet out there like Earth. Why don't we suggest they send scout ships into our area of the galaxy? They have more advanced technology than we have. Maybe they'll find a habitable planet."

"Good idea. Let's talk to the captain and have him send a message to Saros."

The two men got into the elevator and went up two floors to the command center. This was where the junior officers controlled the vital systems on the ship. There was one senior officer in the command center at all times. There they met with Captain Engle.

"Captain, we would like to talk with you," Dale said.

"Okay," he replied. "Come over to my office, and we will talk. James, you have control."

"Yes, sir," responded crewman James.

Inside the small quarters, the three men sat down. "What can you tell me?" Captain Engle asked.

"We are afraid it is bad news. We have encountered the same problem we had on Saros. Either the water cannot be separated from the deadly compound it's joined with, or it's not water at all. It is just solidified nitrogen, ammonia, and methane," Dale explained.

"I'm sorry to hear that. Is there any good news?"

"We are wondering if you would be interested in searching outside our solar system. The Milky Way Galaxy, as we call it, is loaded with stars. There must be a red star somewhere with a planet that would sustain life," Harold explained.

Dale continued, "We don't have the technology to go into space. Just recently, our astronomers located a red star with planets revolving around it. One planet occupies the same position there as Earth does here. Perhaps conditions there are just what you are looking for."

"I do not have the authority to go on a search during this mission. I will have to contact Commander Tammer and get instructions," Captain Engle responded. "My job is to investigate here and get you two back to Earth. Then I am to return to Saros."

"We understand," replied Dale. "Let us know if you get new orders. There are two other scientists aboard who could help you with the search. They could analyze the atmosphere, as well as the surface of a planet, if necessary."

"Thanks. I'll keep that in mind when I talk with Commander Tammer. That will take several hours to complete. Go back to your rooms or the lab if you wish. I will speak with you this evening."

Captain Engle rose and pushed the button to open the door. The three men walked back into the command center. Harold and Dale entered the elevator and returned to the lab.

"We should do a few more experiments. Perhaps we missed something," Dale suggested.

"I think I'll check the computer and see if I recorded that new star discovery. If so, I might be able to locate it using the ship's telescope. I'll be working in my quarters."

"Okay. I'm glad they sent us on a science vessel. This one is very well equipped," Dale said. "See you in a while."

Dale worked with the samples while Harold went back to his room to use his computer. Harold was able to find the recording he had made regarding the red star discovery. From it, he worked out the coordinates of the new star. *Now,* he thought *let's see if the ship's telescope can find it.*

He used the intercom to contact the captain and was given permission to go to the bridge. This was where the senior officers controlled the ship.

Harold pressed the intercom button outside the bridge. "Yes. State your business," a gruff voice demanded.

"Harold Jamison, Earth scientist, with the captain's permission to use the ship's long range telescope," replied Harold.

"We have notification and approval for this visit," the gruff voice responded.

Without a sound, the door slid into the wall. Harold walked through the opening, and the panel slid silently back into place.

There were five senior officers and two junior officers on the bridge. All but two of them were busy at their stations. Captain Engle was talking with another officer.

The gruff voice came from a very big Saronian standing guard by the door. He had a weapon in his hand that he put into a belt holster once he was sure this was Harold and there was no danger.

"Come right over," Captain Engle invited. "We have received permission to look around a little while we are here. Will you help us?"

"Certainly," replied Harold. "What are a few more hours compared to the two years that we have been away from Earth?"

"Then get to work. Lieutenant Wiggins, this is Harold Jamison. You are to help him locate a particular star."

"Yes, sir," replied the lieutenant. "Sit next to me. Give me the information, and I'll put it into the computer. Then a picture will appear on the screen in front of you."

"Here are the coordinates," Harold said as he handed over a piece of paper.

A bright red star appeared on the screen a few seconds later. It was about the size of a silver dollar.

"Can we get any readings from it?" Harold asked.

"Yes." After a few more seconds, a printed spectral analysis popped out of the slot below the screen. The lieutenant was the first to speak. "These readings are similar to the ones from Roo, our own red star. This is unbelievable!"

28

"CAN WE FOCUS ON THE PLANETS?" HAROLD ASKED.

"I can try. I'll only be able to get the ones off to the side and a little behind the star. If they are in front of the star, we'll only see a black spot."

Lieutenant Wiggins typed some more information into the computer. A broader picture came onto the screen. Four smaller dots appeared off to the side of the red star. More typing followed, and then the picture zoomed in on one of the planets near the red star.

"Why did you pick that one?" asked Harold.

"It appears to be the same distance from the sun as Saros is from Roo. I cannot get any more information about it because it is between the red star and us. The only way to learn more is to go there," stated Lieutenant Wiggins. "Captain Engle. Perhaps you should see this, sir."

"Very well," he replied, getting up from his command chair. "What are we looking at?"

"This is the red star the Earth people discovered. Its spectral readings are the same as Roo's. There are planets revolving around it. At least one of them is the same distance from it as Saros is from Roo."

"I must report this to Commander Tammer," Captain Engle said. "How far away is it?"

"I just calculated it, sir. It is approximately 4.3 light-years from here. We do not have the capability to go that far, sir," responded a dejected Lieutenant Wiggins.

"Yes, I understand that. But this discovery is promising. Perhaps you will find a red star that is close enough for us to travel to. Keep looking." Then Captain Engle returned to his command chair.

The two men spent the next hour looking at various sectors of space. There was nothing close that showed any promise.

"This is very frustrating," Harold later told Dale while they were eating in the cafeteria. "There has to be a habitable planet somewhere near either Earth or Saros."

Harold had an answer. "If this were *Star Trek,* we would use trans warp drive and cover those light-years in a few hours. This confirms just how large the universe is."

"Because it is so large and there are so many stars, there must be more planets out there with life on them besides Earth and Saros," Dale concluded.

"I agree. But what if some of it isn't friendly? Look at the threat Saros poses to Earth."

"When we get back, we need to find a way to get our government alerted to the danger it faces," Dale went on.

"There must be some way we can prepare Earth for an invasion. And that scares me because the Saronian technology is far beyond ours."

"I wonder if there is a way to smuggle one of their paralyzer weapons into our stuff when we return to Earth. Then our scientists could learn how it works and either make similar weapons or make a shield to protect us from them."

"And what if we get caught? We've been working with them to help solve their water problem, then we try to steal from them? No thanks."

"I see what you mean," Harold said. "Maybe we should ask for their help. Their government does not want a war with Earth. And the PSSG only wants water to save their planet. If there is an invasion, maybe the legitimate government on Saros will help Earth repel it. We are certainly no match for them alone." Harold thought for a minute and then continued. "You're right. It would be wrong to steal technology. I do think we should ask them about it. What do you think?"

"Yes, we should ask. I don't think we should talk with Captain Engle, though. We should try to speak with Commander Tammer."

"How do we do that now that we have come through the wormhole?" Harold asked.

"I don't think we can. So let's think about it a while and maybe we'll need to talk with Captain Engle after all."

The two men finished their supper and went back to their quarters. They had adjoining rooms on deck three.

Captain Engle had sent another message to Commander Tammer. He told him about the discovery of the red sun and how far away it was. He asked if he should abandon their search and return the scientists to Earth. He needed to know what to do next.

I sure wish I could discover a habitable planet out there somewhere. A war is something I do not want, Captain Engle thought. *Maybe I could use the ship's telescope once we get back closer to Saros near the wormhole. I might locate something in the opposite direction from Saros.*

Then a terrible thought occurred to him. *I wonder if the wormhole can be destroyed. That would stop the PSSG from attacking Earth. I had better talk with Commander Tammer about this when I return.*

His duty shift was ending, so he gave command to his second and retired to his quarters. It was nighttime, and the hall lights had been dimmed. *Perhaps I will have some answers in the morning,* he thought again. *At least, there should be some orders from Commander Tammer by then.*

He turned out the light and went to sleep.

29

DAGNAUT AND JOBLANC WERE NOT HAPPY WITH GENERAL Blubick. Their little cabin in the woods was barely big enough for the two of them. Now, several more had arrived. The general's plan was not a good one according to them.

"This is stupid!" Dagnaut said as he spit on the ground from the edge of the porch. "Kidnapping or killing Dr. M is not going to help at all. He has been living here long enough to make many friends. He must have found others who will help him repel an invasion. I am sure he has a plan that we need to learn about."

"I agree," said Joblanc. "Dr. M will never tell these military men anything. They will end up killing him before they learn anything. We can obtain the information if we just continue to spy on him."

"Right now, we have to find them another place to stay. What do you think about that secluded cabin on the other lake where we ditched those two dead Earth people?"

"That is a good idea."

The two men left their cabin and drove over to the nearby lake. They had a little trouble finding the right road. There were dirt side roads everywhere.

"There is the road," Dagnaut said. "I remember that strange tree with its branches hanging all the way to the ground."

Joblanc turned down that road. The road got narrower, and they stopped just before the road ended. There was a side road going off to the right. It was not quite wide enough for their car.

"This is it," Dagnaut said.

They walked along for about one hundred yards before coming upon the old cabin. It looked the same as when they were there before.

"I will look inside," Joblanc offered. "It still looks deserted."

There was dust and dirt everywhere inside. One window was cracked. The front door was locked. They did not want to break in. They were just looking around.

"I think this will work fine for them. Or if they insist, you and I can move in here."

"I do not want to give up our beds," Dagnaut said. "Maybe we could move them over here. I hope the soldiers are only here for a week like General Blubick said."

"I have a better idea. If we have to move, we can use some of our money to buy new beds."

"I think we should read the local paper and see if anything is available to rent," Dagnaut continued. "We have lots of money. That way we would not have to worry about the owner coming along and having us arrested."

"That is a good idea. We can go into town on the way back. Maybe we can find a cabin we can look at today."

"Slow down," cautioned Dagnaut. "We need to think this through. We have to be able to convince someone to rent to us. We cannot tell them where we are from. We have no references or previous Earth addresses we can use. This might not be easy."

"We can offer a big deposit against any damage that might occur. We need to get some paper and pencils. We already have the new computer. We will tell them we are writers, and we need a rustic cabin setting where we can write."

"Great idea," Dagnaut said as they reached their car. "We will get a newspaper and see if there are any rental brochures at the supermarket or the post office."

There were no houses on the road leading to the trail to the deserted cabin. There were only two cabins in the half mile before that. And there were no cars in either of the driveways.

"If we cannot rent something, then this old cabin will be perfect," Dagnaut concluded.

They picked up three advertisements at the post office and two at the supermarket. Each had a description of a cabin, suggested weekly rent, and a telephone number. They took the advertisements home with them. They could talk about them later.

"I want to be home when Captain Monteford and his men return. I kind of hope they were not able to capture

Dr. M. Of course, they will keep trying if unsuccessful today."

"I am rather tired," Joblanc yawned. "I think I will take a nap." He headed for the back bedroom.

"I will rest here on the couch," Dagnaut replied.

The two men awoke two hours later. It was starting to get dark.

"It is getting late, and they are not back yet," Dagnaut said.

"That was quite a nap. I had a dream someone blew up our cabin…with us inside!" Joblanc exclaimed.

"Well, we are still here. So no one has blown us up yet."

"When do you think the soldiers will return?" Joblanc asked.

"I hope they never return. That would make our lives much easier. Then we could go back to keeping our eyes on Dr. M and that Tessie woman. We could even spy on Henri some. She spends a lot of time at Tessie's house."

"That might be because Tessie is her grandmother, you idiot!" Dagnaut fired back.

The two men made supper, played a card game they had brought from Saros, and went to bed around 10:30. They were still wondering what Captain Monteford and his men were doing when they finally went to sleep.

30

GRAMMA TESSIE BROKE THE SILENCE AS THEY APPROACHED her house. "I don't know about the rest of you, but I'm hungry. It's nearly 12:30. I have some stew I made yesterday. There is also some chocolate cake. I'll put together some lunch as soon as we get inside."

"Good idea," Grams added as she pulled into the driveway. "Everything looks normal here."

"Let's take a few minutes to unwind once we get inside. I know you kids have questions, but follow me to the basement and do not say a word until I tell you to," Dr. M stated.

"Okay," Henri answered.

Tessie unlocked the door, and once they were all inside, she relocked it. "There," she said. "Now, I'll fix some lunch."

"I'll help you," Grams added.

"Dr. M motioned for the kids to follow him. They went down the stairs, and Dr. M led them to the far wall.

Tessie's control room looked just like Grams' room, except that it was quite a bit larger. Dr. M had supervised the building of both rooms. Then he had installed the electronic equipment. This was their main control room.

They would enter the secret room that was located behind the false wall that had been built five feet inside the actual foundation wall of the basement. It looked like the basement ended at this wall that went all the way across the end of the basement. There was a large built-in storage wall unit blocking the door. A hidden lever in it caused the entire unit to swing out two feet from the wall. The hinges were hidden by the decorative woodwork around the unit.

Once the unit moved away from the wall, Dr. M punched in a code on the small pad on the back of the unit. This caused the hidden door to slide into the wall and made an opening for Dr. M and the kids to walk through. He pushed another keypad on the wall inside the room, and the door closed. The wall unit swung back into place. Dr. M pushed a seemingly invisible button on the wall, and power came into the room. Next, he turned on the lights.

"You two can talk or just sit. I need to send a message to Saros. Then I'll leave you two here to talk for a few minutes. Hopefully, things won't turn out like last time."

He got right to work. He powered up the special computer and the long distance communications module he had brought from Saros. An encrypted message explaining the events of the morning was soon on its way to the base on Ganymede. From there, it would be relayed through the wormhole and on to Saros. He would be interested in hearing Commander Tammer's response to the bold move the PSSG had just made.

I'm very lucky these kids were along on this trip, he thought. *I could have been killed along with Grams and Tessie. They have been through a lot today. We will have to spend some time with them and talk them through what has been happening.*

He checked the cameras showing the outside of the house. No one was there. He looked at the digital recording of that morning. No one had approached the house.

I'll bet those spies told the soldiers about me, he thought. *But how come they bugged Tessie's car and followed it? Perhaps they suspected Tessie. I'll have to ask her about that.*

He decided he was finished. "Here are the codes to open the door from inside," he said. "Always check this camera before opening the door." He showed them how to check the camera that showed the entire basement so they could be sure no one was there when they opened the hidden door. "Come upstairs when you've finished talking."

After checking the camera, he entered the code and the doorway opened. He entered the wall unit code into the keypad on the back of the unit, and it swung away from the wall, allowing him to leave. He repeated the process from the outside, and the secret room disappeared. He went upstairs to see how the ladies were doing with lunch.

I will need to look for hidden recording devices the spies might have placed here before I leave, he thought. *I don't want them to hear us talking.*

Tessie and Grams were sitting in the yard facing the lake. Dr. M walked over and joined them.

"Ladies," he said, "I made a discovery just before our meeting at the farm. I met Tessie's niece and her son."

"Who could that be?" Tessie asked. "I don't have any relatives around here."

Dr. M smiled. "Her name is Torah Gotto. She said her parents moved their family away from here many years ago."

"Oh, my," Tessie said. "Where did you meet her? What's she doing in Millville?"

"I met her at the school. She was registering her tenth grade son for fall classes."

"I lost track of her family when they moved away," Tessie added. "I never expected to hear from them again."

"She said she would start work at the manufacturing plant next week. Her son's name is Hunter. He came across as an angry teenager when I met him. He bragged about his running ability, said he didn't like our little town, and he was rude.

"There's something else that disturbed me. He had a very bright Saronian aura. I've never seen one as bright. It could be caused by the yellow sun, or it could be a very serious threat."

"What does that mean?" Grams asked.

"Trouble. There are legends in Saronian history that tell of villains whose skin would glow in the dark. They were evil and very powerful. I hope he's not one of them."

"How will you find out?" Tessie asked.

"We'll wait and see. If he is one of them, it will be easy for us to tell when he starts to do impossible tasks."

"Oh," moaned Tessie. "We don't need this. And in my family, too. Did Torah say anything about contacting me?"

"She said she just arrived in town and was staying at the motel. She wanted to rent an apartment before starting work next week. She mentioned that she knew you lived here on a small lake."

"I'll have to look her up after we get these two families reunited," Tessie concluded.

"I think it's time to finish getting lunch ready," Grams stated.

"Okay. Let's go in, and we can all help," Dr. M said.

. . . .

"Here we are again," J.J. said as he sighed loudly. "We're locked in a soundproof room with a lot of electronic equipment."

"I hope we don't find the same situation upstairs like last time," Henri replied. "I couldn't go through that again."

"You know," J.J. said, "your quick thinking and your necklace probably saved all our lives today. Thank you."

"I hadn't thought of it like that. We do make a good team, don't we?"

"If there is a war coming, we're going to need more weapons than we have now. I wonder what powers the other two kids will have."

"Let's ask Dr. M. We also need to ask about our fathers."

"That's right," J.J. replied. "I hope he has some good answers for us."

"Dr. M said we couldn't talk in the house. That means we'll have to wait until after we eat to ask our questions."

"I am kind of hungry," J.J. admitted.

J.J. checked the surveillance camera in the basement. He put the code into the keypad, and then the doorway opened. Henri entered the code into the back of the bookcase, and it slid away from the wall.

Henri entered the numbers again from the outside, and the door closed. Finally, she pushed the secret lever on the back of the bookcase, and it slid back against the wall.

They climbed the stairs and found lunch spread out on the dining room table. They all sat down and ate.

"Do you kids know what my new job will be in the fall?" Dr. M asked.

"Aren't you teaching sixth grade again?" asked Henri.

"No. I'm moving to the middle school. They want me to be a 7th and 8th grade counselor. I'll get to work with some of the kids I had in class last year."

"That's really cool," J.J. said enthusiastically. "A lot of kids will be happy that you are moving up with them."

"Summer is going fast," Gramma Tessie added. "Tomorrow is Saturday. Do you want to come out for an extra swim?"

"We'd love to," Henri said. "Erika told me yesterday she wanted to ride bikes out here the next time."

"Mike told me a couple of days ago that his mom had volunteered to drive the two of us out next time, but riding bikes sounds like more fun. I'll ask her if she can drive us another time. Is that okay with everybody?" J.J. asked.

"That will be fine," Gramma Tessie said. "I have a new game I want the four of you to try. I think you will like it. Grams and I played it last week."

"Okay," Henri said. "Then we'll all be here tomorrow morning."

"Great!" Gramma Tessie replied. "I bought some hamburger and potato salad yesterday. I think I'll bake an apple pie this afternoon. Grams, will you help me with it?"

"I sure will," she replied. "Do you need any ingredients from town?"

"I think everything we need is right here."

Dr. M spoke up next. "Let's take the dishes to the kitchen. Then let's take a walk down by the lake. Maybe we'll see some geese."

They all helped clear the table and put away the food. When they had finished, Dr. M motioned for them to quietly go downstairs. He opened and loudly closed the outside door.

Once in the basement, Gramma Tessie repeated the steps to open the hidden doorway. Within a minute, they were all comfortably seated in the soundproof basement control room.

"Okay, kids," Dr. M stated. "Let's hear it."

Henri blurted it out first. "We want to know about our dads. Are they alive? Where are they? What are they doing?" Tears began to run down her cheeks. Her voice quivered as she tried to continue.

"Here, dear," Gramma Tessie said, giving her a tissue. She got up and took a few steps over to Henri who also stood and rushed into Tessie's outstretched arms. "You poor girl. Both of you have been through a lot today."

"Oh, Gramma," she cried, "why did our dads disappear?" She continued to sob as the tears continued to flow. "And Dr. M just murdered six people and destroyed Grams' home and your car. I'm scared and confused."

"Me, too," added J.J. before Tessie could answer Henri. He was fighting back the tears, too. But he was a boy and wanted to be brave in front of Henri. "Tell us what you know about our dads, please. Will we ever see them again?" He barely got the words out. A tear started down his cheek, but he deftly used a tissue to blow his nose and intercept it.

"The three of us know where your dads are and what they have been doing," Dr. M stated. "Now is the perfect time for this revelation. Your dads have been working for the governments of two worlds. They were selected by the President of the United States and supported by the ruling government of Saros.

"It was not safe to tell you where they were until now. As I told you, Saros is a dying planet. Your dads were asked to help. They did not have to go. And, at first, they didn't want to. But when they learned what was at stake and that they could help, they volunteered."

"So where are they?" J.J. asked once again, gaining his composure.

"Because of their knowledge and expertise in physics and chemistry, they went to Saros," Dr. M continued. "It was originally planned for them to stay only one year. However, they made enough discoveries, and their work showed such promise that they stayed until they had done all they could."

"I don't see why we weren't told," Henri said. "We can keep a secret."

"This was too big a secret for any of you to have to try to keep. Even your mothers weren't told. Can you imagine how that made Grams and me feel?" Gramma Tessie asked. Now, her eyes were tearing up. "We had to lie to our families. It was very difficult to do."

"No one could learn about the threat from Saros, and that aliens had landed on Earth," Grams added. "Can you imagine the panic?"

"We didn't think Earth was ready to believe in life on other planets. We're sure people are not ready to be threatened with interplanetary war. There would be widespread panic," Dr. M explained. "No one wanted your families to have that responsibility.

"I just heard from Captain Engle. He is commanding a ship that is now on the far side of Neptune. Your fathers are on board. They will return to Earth tomorrow. They have been surveying there as well as looking for distant planets that could support Saronian life."

"You can be very proud of your fathers," Grams continued. "Their work has extended life on Saros for at least another two decades."

"How are we going to explain our dads returning after being gone for over two years?" J.J. asked.

Dr. M responded, "That has already been taken care of. Your fathers have been working with Commander Tammer on Saros to come up with an explanation. General Stromburg has been discussing the same thing with the president. I think they have come up with a reasonable explanation."

Some of the color was returning to Henri's cheeks. "Can we tell our moms?" she asked. "Will we really see our dads in two days? I can't wait!"

"We are quite sure it will be tomorrow," Dr. M continued. "They have to land some place away from here. Then the story needs to be released, and they'll be transported home. That's all I have been told. You may tell your mothers and brothers, but no one else."

Henri seemed to have forgotten her comment about the murdered men. Dr. M was glad to let that topic rest for the time being. He thought he could explain it, but he would like to do it when only Henri and J.J. were present.

"Can we go home now?" asked Henri. "I can't wait to tell Mom."

"Me, too," J.J. added. "Will you drive us, Grams?"

"I have already called both your mothers," Gramma Tessie said. "They will be here with your brothers in a few minutes. I told them you were having a celebration, and you both wanted them here."

"This will be some celebration!" shouted J.J. "Wow! Seeing Dad again after two years. I knew he would return home someday. I never dreamed he was on another planet millions of miles from Earth, though."

You'll only have one day for your reunion before we meet the press," Dr. M added. "I ran a sweep, and there are microphones hidden in three of the rooms upstairs. I'll disable them and erase their contents after we finish down here."

"I'll go upstairs and get us all something to drink while we wait for your moms," Gramma Tessie offered.

"Let me check the camera first," Dr. M said. After a few seconds, he said, "All clear."

Tessie entered the codes and went out through the small doorway. Grams went with her to help.

This was planned in order for Dr. M to have some time with Henri and J.J. There was a lot to explain to them.

Dr. M closed the doorway from the inside and looked at Henri and J.J. "You two have grown up quite a bit today," he started out. "I am very proud of both of you."

31

THE KIDS STARED BACK AT DR. M. THEY DIDN'T KNOW WHAT to say.

"You two worked together to save our lives today," praised Dr. M. "I'm not sure you realize that."

"We were talking about that," J.J. responded. "Were those soldiers that mean? Would they have tortured us or even killed us?"

"They would have done both in order to get the information they wanted. There may be a war back on Saros between the two factions. If the PSSG wins, and I think they might, then there will be a war with Earth."

"What does that mean?" Henri asked. "What is happening on Saros?"

"The PSSG is gaining more support every day," Dr. M continued. "The longer the government is unable to find more water, the more people will be turned against it. It's a matter of survival.

"Your fathers were a big help. It's too bad they couldn't find a way to use the water on one of the moons. With only a couple of decades left before we run out of water, the people will soon become desperate."

"What can we do to help?" Henri asked. "We're just kids."

"Yes, you are kids. But you are kids with special powers. Once we get the other two kids united with their Saros stones, we'll stand a better chance of winning the war."

"Who are the other two kids?" J.J. asked. "When will you contact them?"

"You are going to contact them," Dr. M responded.

"We don't know who they are," Henri stated. "Are you going to tell us their names?"

"They'll be here tomorrow to swim," Dr. M replied with a big smile on his face.

Once again, Henri and J.J. were flabbergasted! They looked at each other and then back at Dr. M. No one said a word.

Henri finally spoke. "Mike and Erika?" she asked incredulously.

"Yes. Don't you think the four of you will make a good team?" Dr. M asked.

"At least, they are two kids we know and like," Henri said, still amazed. She was in disbelief.

"How will we tell them?" J.J. wondered.

Henri had an answer. "Hey, you two. We just found out we were born from aliens, and our dads have been on a far away planet for the past two years. We can stop time and turn time back an hour and relive it, making changes if we want to."

J.J. continued with the fun. He added, "You two are also related to aliens and are about to receive some special powers, too."

"They'll laugh at us. They'll think we've lost our minds!" Henri concluded. And then she laughed. "It is pretty funny."

Dr. M just sat and smiled. Laughter was good medicine. It would relieve the stress J.J. and Henri had been feeling.

"We could give them a demonstration of our powers," Henri suggested.

"Yes," J.J. replied. "And when I turn time back, they won't remember anything."

"I could stop time and then touch them, so they could wake up and see everything frozen," Henri said. "That would amaze them."

Finally, Dr. M spoke. "Slow down, you two," he said. "It does sound quite preposterous the way you stated it. However, there is some truth in what you just said."

"What would that be?" J.J. asked.

"Mike and Erika are the great-grandchildren of the first group that J.J.'s great-grandfather brought to Earth. Mike and Erika both have Saronian fathers and Earth mothers. What do you think of that?" Dr. M concluded.

"Wow!" Henri exclaimed.

"Double wow!" exclaimed J.J.

The kids were ready to ask more questions when Dr. M stood up. "Okay," he said. "I have the last two special Saros stones. I brought them here from the Cave of the Mystics on Saros. Grams, Tessie, and I agree that Mike and Erika are the other two the prophecies predicted."

"So what will their powers be? What will we tell them to convince them to join us?" J.J. asked.

"First, let's talk with your mothers and get them on board. We don't need to tell them about your powers yet," Dr. M stated. "They will have enough to deal with when they hear their husbands are returning to them."

"What are you going to tell our mothers?" J.J. asked.

"Your fathers are coming home in good health. We are going to tell their wives the truth. This was a very important mission they have been on at the request of the President of the United States. Knowing that their husbands had ties to Saros, I wonder if the wives might have suspected the truth. I must ask them to tell no one where their husbands have been.

"We're going to tell everyone else a much different story. We'll say they contracted a very deadly disease. It was unbelievably dangerous and contagious. They had to be completely isolated immediately. There was no hope of them surviving unless we put them in an experimental unit being developed at a secret military base. The doctors there have been working for a couple of years with just-discovered spores and microscopic organisms brought up from the ocean depths.

"There is some potential mental failure resulting from this disease. We will say that all the family members had been scanned at your doctor's office just over two years ago to be sure they were not infected. The test results came back negative. But with the possibility of mental problems, we did not want word of this getting out to the public. If any of you had known about the disease and then let it slip or had a mental breakdown and talked about it, a dangerous panic would have ensued.

"A cure was finally developed while Dale and Harold were kept alive in their cryogenic-freeze isolation chambers. They are now cured and are not a danger to others."

"Do you think the town will believe this?" J.J. wanted to know.

"We will have two well-known doctors from the Serco/Cryo Health Group explain everything. Their group is known worldwide for the advancements they have made in medicine. They have a reputation for solving mysterious disease cases and handling rare communicable diseases. I think most people will believe them. We will try to keep this as local as possible."

"When will this take place?" Henri asked.

"Hopefully, in two days," Dr. M said. "The ship will land tomorrow. The Serco doctors are already in town. They will make a short presentation to the newspaper at ten o'clock the day after tomorrow. Your fathers will meet with them before the news conference. That will help them to know what to say.

"There will be a lot of amnesia on their part regarding the last two years or so of their lives."

"I think that will work," Henri commented.

"Now, I will check outside and see if anyone is in the basement," Dr. M said. A few seconds later, he announced, "All clear. Let's go upstairs. I think we can talk down by the lake. Don't say anything about this inside the house."

"Okay," they both responded.

Dr. M opened the secret doorway, and the three of them exited the room. Dr. M closed the door and pushed the lever to put the wall unit back into place before they went upstairs.

There was no one in the house when they got upstairs. They could see four people sitting in lawn chairs down by the lake. The moms had arrived.

Both J.J. and Henri ran down to their moms and hugged them. They both blurted out at the same time, "Dad's coming home the day after tomorrow!"

"What? That can't be!" Mrs. Jamison exclaimed.

"How's that possible? Where have they been?" asked an equally astonished Mrs. Matthews. "Who told you this?"

"I told them," Dr. M said. "Your husbands have been doing world-saving research on Saros. The planet their great-grandfathers came from is dying from a water shortage. Your husbands have given Saros twenty more years to look for a solution. The President of the United States asked them to go with the approval of the governing body of Saros. We are very sorry we couldn't tell you, and that it has taken so long. They were supposed to be returned to Earth after one year. Their work took much longer than anyone thought. Please accept our thanks and the apologies of the Saros government."

"This is too much," cried Mrs. Jamison as she hugged J.J.

"I can't believe it. Is it really true?" Mrs. Matthews asked as she fiercely hugged Henri. Tears were streaming down her face.

"Yes, it's true," confirmed Dr. M. "There's a small news conference the day after tomorrow at the health clinic on Main Street in Millville."

Then Mrs. Matthews hugged Mrs. Jamison, and they cried together.

"Let's all sit down, and I will explain as much as I can," Dr. M suggested.

They all sat in lawn chairs by the lake as Dr. M explained to the mothers some of what he had told Henri and J.J. in the basement.

They seemed satisfied and started to talk about a celebration. No one was sure where and when to celebrate.

"Why don't we have both families come out here tomorrow for a barbeque and swim party?" Gramma Tessie suggested. "We can eat and talk and swim. I'm sure there will be a lot to catch up on."

"That's for sure," Mrs. Jamison said as she wiped her face with her handkerchief.

"I think that is a great idea," Mrs. Matthews added.

"Wait a minute," J.J. said. "Didn't you say they were returning the day after tomorrow?"

"That's when the town gets the information," Dr. M explained. "They will be here at the lake tomorrow morning. You will all see them then. You will all spend the night here tonight and tomorrow and go to the news conference together on Sunday."

"Tomorrow is Saturday, Grams," J.J. said. "Mike and Erika are coming out to swim."

"That's all part of the plan. You four kids will have some time to spend together. I would also like to talk with the four of you while the adults get reacquainted," Dr. M said. Then he winked at J.J. and Henri.

"I don't think I will be able to sleep tonight," Henri said.

"You'd better," J.J. commented. "Tomorrow is a very big day."

"I'd better call Erika and tell her that our families are spending the night at the lake. She and Mike can meet us here around 1:00 tomorrow."

"I'll call Mike and tell him the same thing," J.J. added. "He and Erika can work out their plans to get here."

"Here comes Jerry," J.J. announced. "What should we tell him?"

"Nothing," Dr. M instructed. "He and Joey can find out tomorrow when their fathers get here."

"Hi, everybody," greeted Jerry. "What're you doing?"

"Just talking about having a big swim party tomorrow," Mrs. Jamison answered. "Where's Joey?"

"He's using the bathroom. He'll be right out. Can he come to the swim party, too?"

"Sure," his mom replied. "We're going to have a fantastic party. What would you think of spending tonight here at the lake?"

"That would be great! Is Joey spending the night, too? Can we sleep in the same bedroom?"

"I'm sure we can work that out," Gramma Tessie said.

32

SATURDAY MORNING, JOBLANC AND DAGNAUT AWOKE AND ate breakfast. They had a lot on their minds.

"They are not back yet," Dagnaut said. "Do you think something happened to them?"

"Captain Stamtu told us to be careful around Dr. M. He has a lot of respect for him. Do you suppose he got the better of Captain Monteford and his five goons?" remarked Joblanc.

"That would be fine with me. I never want to see them again!"

"We could drive into town and look for them. Perhaps they got lost and are waiting for us."

"Okay. If we do not locate them by evening, I think we should send a message to Captain Stamtu."

"That is a good plan. We can shop and have lunch in town. Then we can drive around a little. A drive past Dr. M's house would be wise. We can download the recordings from his house. We might learn something."

"If there is no news there, we will take a ride over to that Tessie woman's house," Dagnaut suggested. "We can listen to her recordings, too. Someone must know something."

The two men cleaned up from breakfast and then took a short walk. They didn't go far as they hoped to avoid anyone who lived nearby.

Upon returning to the cabin, they both were thinking the same thing. "We need to rent a cabin. Then we would not have to sneak around and worry about getting caught where we should not be," Dagnaut stated. "I want to look at those rental advertisements again."

"How much money do we have?" asked Joblanc.

Dagnaut went to the money drawer and pulled out the piece of paper. It contained an accounting of their money. "We have $279,000 left. We should open a savings and checking account after we register at the motel on the edge of town. That will give us an address. It will also keep our money safe."

"Good. Now, we need to make up some Earth names." Joblanc was quick with words. He had learned English very fast. "I will be Joe Blanc. You can be Dag Nauton. These will be easy names for us to remember, and they sound more like Earth names."

"Very good," Dagnaut complimented. "I like my new name. Now, some of this money should be hidden in case someone comes in here while we are gone. There is a metal box in the bedroom closet. We will bury it away from the house in a place where only we can find it."

"Okay. We do have a lot of cash according to Earth standards. Perhaps we should drive into the larger town of Davisburg and put some money in some of its banks. We might arouse suspicion if we put a large amount of money in just one bank."

"I think $140,000 would be the right amount for the Millville bank. We will say we sold some property and are thinking about settling here. We might add that we are also looking for work. Maybe we can find part-time jobs to fit in while watching Dr. M," Dagnaut continued. "If we get jobs, we might be able to rent a cabin without any identification."

"Maybe we can get a picture identification card made when we deposit money at the bank," Joblanc said. "We can tell them we lost everything in a fire, and that we are kind of family outcasts. We want to start over without family interference. We can be cousins. I am tired. I think I will take a nap."

"Okay," replied Dag Nauton. "I will find a safe place to bury the money box. I will show you where it is when you wake up."

A couple of hours later, Joe Blanc woke up. It was 12:30, and he was hungry.

"So, you finally woke up," Dag said. "Come outside. I want to show you something."

Joe put on his shoes, and they went outside.

Dag pointed to two trees growing close together. "See those two tall trees?"

"Yes."

"Walk right in the middle between them. Then stop. Take fifteen steps and you should be right up to another tree. Go five steps to your right and another tree will be in your way. Turn left and walk another fifteen steps. You should see another tree in front of you. Next to it is a bush. I buried the box under the bush and then threw pine needles all over the area," concluded Dag.

"Okay. Fifteen steps from between the two trees, five steps to the right, and fifteen steps to the left. I found it!" Joe exclaimed. "Is it buried under this bush?"

"Yes. Now, we can go rent a room at the motel. Then we will try to put some money in a bank."

They had a little trouble renting a room. The person in charge wanted to see a picture identification card. Finally, Dag said, "You have a lot of empty rooms here. We will pay you a $200 bonus if you rent us a room with two double beds. Better yet, rent us two rooms with a door between. We will also pay a $200-nonrefundable damage deposit if you give us a good monthly rate."

The clerk was the co-owner of the motel, and the deal was too good to pass up. He cut the daily rate by one-third. Dag paid him in cash for two rooms for one month.

They decided to go back to the cabin and bring an extra set of clothes to leave at the motel. They were back in town in an hour. They put their clothes in their rooms and stopped back at the motel office.

"Where would we go if we were looking for work?" Dag asked the clerk.

"What kind of work are you looking for?" he replied.

"Anything. We would like only part-time to start," Dag explained.

"There are two lakes close to town. You might ask at the boat dock or the food store there. They might need some help, or they might know of some other jobs. There is a small manufacturing plant on the south end of town. You might try there, too."

"Thanks," Dag said. "Is the bank open?"

"Yes," replied the clerk.

"Good," Dag said. "We want to open a savings account."

"Don't bother," the clerk responded. "They will require two photo IDs. Since you don't have any, they will ask you a lot of questions. They might even call the police."

"We do not want that," Dag replied. "We are not crooks. We just want to get a fresh start away from our families. We will find another place for our money."

"Perhaps I can help," the clerk went on. "There's a built-in safe in each of your rooms. I have a large safe in my office for other valuables."

"Thank you," Dag said. "Joe and I will decide what to do later."

The two men breathed a sigh of relief when they got back to their rooms. "We could have been in trouble if the police had been called to investigate us at the bank. Even though we have not committed a crime that they know about, we cannot explain where we are from," Joe said.

"We should see how much money we can get into our room safes," Dag suggested.

They were able to put $40,000 into each safe. They hid $21,000 in the trunk of their car. Dag would bury the rest back at the cabin.

"Okay. I think we should buy a box while we are in town. Then we can go back to the cabin and bury it in a separate place," Joe suggested.

"I like that. Then our money will be spread around. If we need money and cannot get to one place, we can go to one of the others."

They left the motel and went to one of the restaurants in town and had lunch. Then they went to the big grocery store and bought a plastic container with a tight fitting lid. Finally, they headed for the deserted cabin.

There was an empty cabin on a road near where they had been staying. They used the 15x5x15 code again and found another easy-to-remember place to bury the second box. They retrieved the extra money from the car's trunk and buried it.

"I hope there are no soldiers waiting for us," Dag said as they drove back to their cabin. He was not disappointed. The place was just as they had left it. They went inside to talk.

"I think it is time to contact Captain Stamtu," Joe said. "I hope those soldiers do not return while we are waiting for a reply."

"I will get the scanner from the attic where we hid it. That is how we discovered where Dr. M was after our ship used their big scanner from space."

"Good idea. Our scanner will pick them up if they are within one hundred miles."

They went into the bedroom and pulled down the folding stairs. Joe climbed up and uncovered the scanner. He handed it down to Dag. He also handed down their weapons. They had hidden them in the attic while they were away from the cabin. They did not want the owner to find them in case he returned to check on his property.

It only took a moment to start the scanner. The battery was still strong, and within a minute, they had a blip. However, it was only one blip and was a few miles away.

"There should be more blips," Joe stated. "It registers one blip for each Saronian it finds."

"Yes. Captain Monteford and his men are more than one hundred miles away. What could they be doing?"

"I do not know. At least, we have something to report to Captain Stamtu."

"Do we assume the blip on the screen is Dr. M?" Joe asked.

"It is either him, or one of the soldiers was left behind, and they have taken Dr. M away somewhere."

"We should drive to Dr. M's house. Perhaps we will get lucky and see him."

"Okay. First, I will put this scanner back in the attic. We will get the radio down when we get back. Put the weapons in the car's trunk for now," Dag said.

It took twenty minutes to get through all the twists and turns of the many narrow roads from where their cabin was. They made good time once they got on the main road.

"Drive by at a normal speed," Joe said.

"I know. We do not want to attract attention. Look! That is Dr. M on the front walk."

Dr. M was walking along the sidewalk leading to his house. He had his mail in his hands and was looking down at it. He did not see the spies drive past. At least, that was what Joe and Dag thought.

"Keep going. Turn at the next corner," Dag ordered.

"It is all right. He does not know what our car looks like."

"Well, that settles it. Something has happened to Captain Monteford and his men. Now we can notify Captain Stamtu."

"Do you think we should wait a few more days before we send that message?" Joe asked. "They may have found a hiding place and are waiting to kidnap Dr. M. It will be better to wait until the weeklong mission is over. Then we can report what we have learned."

"Okay. You are right. Can we go home now?"

"Sure. I will stop and get some takeout at that restaurant on the edge of town."

. . . .

Dr. M had not only seen the car as the spies drove past, he recognized it from his surveillance recording.

What are they up to? He wondered. *They are probably looking for those six soldiers. They will need to report them missing soon. They can't think I overpowered six men, so they are most likely puzzled. Good. That will give us more time to get organized.*

33

VERY EARLY SATURDAY MORNING, AN INVISIBLE SHIP entered an orbit around Earth. Captain Engle said thank you to Dale and Harold as they entered the small craft that would take them to the surface. It was 4:00 a.m. when they set foot back on Earth for the first time in a little over two years. Dr. M was there to meet them at an isolated spot forty-five miles northwest of Millville.

"Welcome home," Dr. M greeted.

"Thanks. It's good to be back on Earth again," sighed Dale.

"I don't ever want to leave again," added Harold.

"You won't have to," Dr. M said. "You have done all you can."

"Are you taking us home?" Dale asked.

"No. I'm taking you to Tessie's house by the lake. Both of your families are there waiting for you. You will spend the rest of today and tomorrow there, and then we will go into town to meet the press Sunday at 1:00 p.m. The two Serco/Cryo Health Group doctors will come out to Tessie's to talk with you tomorrow morning. You can get your stories ready for the news conference."

"Do our children know we are alive and coming home?" Harold asked.

"J.J. and Henri know. I told them yesterday. Your wives also know. You can surprise Jerry and Joey.

"We had a rather unfortunate run-in with six soldiers from Saros. The PSSG sent them to capture me. Actually, their orders were to capture Tessie and Henri also. We were to be tortured and killed, unless I told them the defensive plans Earth was making for their invasion. They also wanted the magno-pulse machine I keep on Earth."

"Why would they want Tessie and Henri tortured?" a concerned Dale asked. "They don't know anything."

"A lot has changed in the past few months," Dr. M cautioned. "There are three spies living near here from Saros. They are watching me. They must be living someplace near Tessie.

"Tessie and Henri went for a boat ride awhile ago to a new beach Tessie had ordered constructed. While they were there, Tessie told Henri about a special Saros stone. It's been handed down in Tessie's family. Henri is the next owner. Henri is one of four kids born on Earth of Saronian ancestry who are mentioned in a very old prophecy. I just reviewed the prophecy in the Cave of the Alugets on Saros. Harold, J.J. is also one of the selected ones. There is also a Saros stone that has been handed down in your family. I won't go into detail now as I want the kids to tell you their own stories.

"One of the spies overheard Tessie telling Henri about the Saros stone when she gave it to her. It was just a fluke accident that this spy happened to see the boat coming across the lake and was able to get in position to overhear them. He did not see Tessie give the stone to Henri. He only heard part of the end of their conversation.

"The mention of the Saros stone made the spies suspicious. They must have decided to watch Tessie, and maybe even Henri. We have been very careful since then," Dr. M concluded.

"What do these Saros stones do?" Dale asked.

"I would rather you hear that from your kids. After you have had time together, I will talk with the four of you. There is a special room in Tessie's basement where we can have complete privacy.

"I wasn't going to tell you all of this until later. You need to reunite with your families first. The presence of these soldiers and the three spies has changed things."

"Where are the soldiers?" Harold asked.

"They are gone. And I am sorry to say, so is your great-grandfather's farmhouse," Dr. M said wistfully.

"What do you mean?" Harold asked.

"We had no choice. They had captured Tessie, Grams, and me. They were planning to torture us for information and then kill us. They were also about to capture J.J. and Henri. To make a long story short, J.J. and Henri saved our lives. Afterward, I had to destroy the farmhouse and the six soldiers," a grim Dr. M stated.

"How did our kids save your lives?" Dale asked. "That seems impossible."

"You will have to wait and hear that from J.J. and Henri later today. Now, let's get you to Tessie's house. It's nearly 4:30. We should arrive there around 6:00 a.m. We can sneak you in through the side door and into the basement. There is a bedroom there with two cots for you. You can sleep there if you are able until everyone is up. Then we can have a big reunion with breakfast.

"If we are discovered by the kids, the reunion can start earlier. They will probably wake everyone up if they see you two."

"That would be fine with me," Dale said. "I can hardly wait to see Harriet and Henri and Joey."

"The sooner the better," joined in Harold. "J.J., Jerry, and Janice must look a little different after more than two years."

"You will find out in just a few hours. Please do not mention the Saros stones. Your wives and the younger brothers know nothing about them. I'd like to keep it that way!" stated Dr. M. "I'll explain later."

Silence filled the car as they drove on through the early morning darkness to Tessie's place. It was still dark when they arrived, but sunrise was very near.

They were able to sneak into the basement unseen. The fathers were tired from their space flight and went right to sleep. Dr. M entered the secret room next to the basement bedroom and sent a message to Saros. Then he slipped into the comfortable chair at the end of the room and dozed for a couple of hours.

The alarm on his watch awakened him at 9:00 a.m. He rubbed the sleep from his eyes and checked the basement camera. The room was empty, so he opened the secret door. He stepped out of the small room and closed the door, and the big storage unit slid back into place. He peeked in on Dale and Harold. They were still asleep. Quietly, he went upstairs.

"Good morning," Tessie greeted him. "Ready for some breakfast?"

"Sure. Is that bacon I smell? I think I smell pancakes, too."

"It sure is. I've been up since eight o'clock, getting things ready for breakfast. We have a lot of people to feed."

"I see the table is all set. Good morning, Grams," Dr. M said as he entered the dining room.

"Good morning," she replied.

"Do I smell bacon?" came J.J.'s voice from the top of the stairs.

"I smell it, too," chorused Henri, Mrs. Matthews, and Mrs. Jamison. They all came downstairs together.

"What's all the noise about?" asked Jerry and Joey as they came around the corner from the downstairs bedroom they shared.

"It's time for breakfast," replied Mrs. Jamison.

Grams and Tessie went to the kitchen while everyone else sat down. They returned with large plates of pancakes, bacon, fried potatoes, and scrambled eggs. On their second trip, they brought orange juice and steaming hot coffee.

For the next half hour or so, they ate and talked and ate some more.

"That was delicious," Dr. M complimented Tessie. "Perhaps the rest of us can help with the next meal."

Suddenly, two familiar voices sounded from the basement doorway. "Is there any food left for us?" asked Dale and Harold as they made their entrance.

"Dad!" yelled J.J., Henri, Jerry, and Joey all at once.

"Harold!" exclaimed Janice.

"Dale!" shouted Harriet.

The four kids rushed to their dads and hugged them fiercely. And then the tears of joy began to fall. No one was spared.

After hugging the kids, the husbands and wives hugged and kissed. No one wanted to let go. And no one could stop crying.

"I'll bet those spies will wonder what all this noise is about," whispered Tessie.

"No, they won't," Dr. M answered. "I disconnected all three microphones. I'll reconnect them in a couple of days after things calm down."

There was so much to tell and so much to ask. They spent the next hour hugging and talking. Grams, Tessie, and Dr. M went out on the back porch facing the lake while the family reunion continued.

"Wasn't that a beautiful sight?" Grams asked.

"It sure was," Tessie returned. "This is the easy part. Let's hope dealing with the press goes as well."

"I'm sure it will," Dr. M replied. "The amnesia will be the answer to nearly every question. The medical people will handle their end with professionalism. They know what they can and cannot say. They will take the heat if there is any."

After nearly an hour, Grams said, "Perhaps we should go back in and clear off the table."

"Yes," agreed Tessie. "We all can help."

"Mike and Erika will be here soon," Dr. M said. "They are in for an interesting afternoon."

When they got back to the dining room, the two families had divided and were talking and smiling. It looked like everything was going to be all right.

34

ERIKA AND MIKE HAD NO IDEA THEIR LIVES WERE ABOUT TO be changed forever.

"I'm so glad that class is finished," Erika said, letting out a long sigh. "It will help me when I take algebra, but I don't like to have to take a class in the summer."

"I understand," Mrs. Sorenson replied. "But you're better prepared now. And now, you can relax and enjoy the rest of the summer."

"You're right, Mom. I still have lots of summer left to have fun with no homework and no schedule. I think I'll sleep until noon tomorrow."

Just then, the phone rang. It was Henri asking if Erika wanted to swim tomorrow.

"So you're going out to Gramma Tessie's to swim tomorrow?" asked Mr. Sorenson.

"Yes. I'd better call Mike and make arrangements."

"Isn't there a big party out there next weekend, too?" asked Mrs. Sorenson.

"Yes," Erika replied. "You and Dad are invited to that one. We plan to be back in town early that evening for the fireworks."

"What time do you want to go?" Mrs. Sorenson wondered.

"Let's leave here at eleven."

"Okay," her mom replied.

A few minutes later, Erika walked out to her backyard to call Mike.

"Hello," Mike answered.

"Hi, Mike. This is Erika. How're you?"

"Hi, Erika. I'm okay. I just came in from playing basketball with Harold next door. What's up?"

"I'm calling about tomorrow. Henri called and wants us to go to Gramma Tessie's to swim."

"Sure, the four of us can hang out down by the lake."

"Henri suggested that you and I ride our bikes out like last time."

"Okay. Where do you want to meet?"

"Ride over to my house at 12:30. It'll take us about a half an hour to ride out there. I'll call Henri back and set the time with her."

"Okay. I'll be at your house at 12:30 tomorrow. See ya then."

"I'll be waiting. Bye, Mike."

"Bye, Erika."

Erika walked back into the house and told her parents that plans had been made for her and Mike to leave her house at 12:30 tomorrow. They would ride their bikes out to Gramma Tessie's house.

"I think I'll read for a while in my room," Erika announced.

"Okay. Dad and I are going to the hardware and the grocery store. Do you need anything?"

"No, thanks. See you later." Erika went down the hall and into her room.

Meanwhile, Mike didn't know what to do. As he walked into the kitchen to get a drink of water, an idea came to him. *I haven't run for a while,* he thought. *I think I'll go for a run.*

He pulled out his cell phone and called J.J. After several rings, it went to voice mail. Mike decided not to leave a message. He tried a couple more of his friends, but no one answered.

"Well," he said, "I'll run alone." He went into his room and changed into some running clothes. He had a nearly new pair of running shoes. *Time to try these out again,* he thought.

He spent nearly ten minutes outside stretching. Then he took off. *I'll run to the middle school first,* he thought. *Then I'll circle the track four times. If I run down to the car dealership on my way home, that will make three miles.*

So off he went. Mike was a good runner. It had been a few months, but he used to run five miles every Saturday morning when the weather was good.

Things went well at first. He covered the distance to the school quickly even though he jogged all the way. Next, he jogged three times around the track. *Time to pick it up,* he thought.

But before he could speed up, another kid suddenly came up from behind and passed him. Mike couldn't believe it. The kid slowed down and let Mike catch up.

"Is that as fast as you can run?" he asked.

"I just jogged a mile and a half. I was about to speed up for the last lap. Who are you?" Mike questioned.

"Call me Hunter," came the reply. "Dr. Emory told me the school had very good running teams."

"I'm Mike. I'm starting seventh grade this year. Cross-country starts on August 20 for middle and high school."

"Well, I hope you can run a lot faster than you just did. Let's see what you've got. I'll race you around the track once."

"Okay. But I'm a little tired and cross-country is about distance, not speed."

"I don't want to hear excuses. Do you want to go two or three laps then?"

"No. One will be enough. Are you ready?"

"I'm always ready. You take off first, and I'll start right after you do."

"Okay." Mike started running and left Hunter standing there. *I won't start out too fast,* he thought. *I'll save my speed for the last 100 yards.*

Hunter took off and easily caught up with Mike. He kept about six or seven yards behind him. *This guy can't run at all,* Hunter thought. *I'll stay a little behind him and fly past at the finish.*

Mike ran at three-quarters speed until he rounded the last curve. With 100 yards left, he gave it everything he had.

Hunter laughed as he easily stayed a few steps behind Mike.

"I can walk faster than this," he laughed. "You're no runner!" he mocked.

Mike tried to go a little faster as he neared the finish line. *I'll show him,* he thought.

Hunter sped up and breezed by Mike with twenty yards left. He won by ten yards, laughing all the way.

"Hey, you can really run. The coaches would love to have you on one of the teams this year."

"I don't run for no coach. Everything I do is for me. So long, slowpoke." Hunter took off so fast Mike was left staring at him until he disappeared around a corner.

"Wow! That's the fastest kid I've ever seen," Mike said out loud. "He's the rudest kid, too. I wonder where he came from." *Well, I'd better finish my run,* he thought.

He jogged along the sidewalk, heading for the car dealership on the edge of town. The dealership came into view as he turned a corner. Also ahead were two men walking on the sidewalk. He figured they had the right-of-way, so he swerved into the yard just before he got to them.

A blur rushed past him. It was Hunter. He ran across Mike's path so closely that he nearly hit Mike. Mike stumbled and went flying off his feet. Luckily, he landed in the grass.

"Ha, ha, ha," Hunter's laughter filled the air. "Now I know you can't run!" He took off before Mike could say anything.

The two men stopped, turned around, and looked at Mike. They walked over to where he was lying on the grass, rubbing his ankle.

"Are you okay?" one of them asked.

"Sure. I just tripped over that idiot's foot! Who does he think he is? Oh, thank you for stopping."

"Can you walk?" the other man asked.

"I think so. My ankle is a little sore. I twisted it when I fell."

"Mike! What happened?" asked a lady who came walking across the street. "I was coming out to sweep the walk when I saw you fall!" she exclaimed. "Who was that kid who ran off?"

"I'm okay, Mrs. Mitchell. I just tripped. It's nothing serious."

"Who are these men?" she asked suspiciously.

"They were just walking along the sidewalk. I ran into the yard to avoid them, and this new kid tripped me."

"What a brat! I don't recognize you," she said to the men. "Are you two new in town?"

"Yes, ma'am. We just took a couple of rooms at the motel. We are thinking of settling here, and we are out walking and looking for work," one of the men explained.

"I'm Mrs. Mitchell. My husband, Bill, owns the McDonald's on Broad Street."

"Nice to meet you. I am Dag and he is Joe."

"Nice to meet you, too. Thank you for offering to help Mike."

"No problem," Dag replied.

"We had better be on our way," Joe said.

"Stop by the McDonald's and ask if they're hiring," suggested Mrs. Mitchell. "You never know when someone decides to quit, and they're left shorthanded."

"Thank you, ma'am. We will be sure to do that," Dag said as they started to walk away.

"Are you sure you're okay, Mike?" Mrs. Mitchell asked.

Mike was still sitting on the ground, rubbing his ankle. "We'll know in a minute when I try to stand up."

He was a little wobbly, but the more he walked around, the better it felt. "I'll be okay. I think I'll be walking the rest of the way home."

"Nonsense. Walk across the street to my house. I'll drive you home. It's too far for you to walk with a sore ankle. You might cause more damage."

"Okay," Mike said giving in. He knew there was no arguing with Mrs. Mitchell.

It only took her a few minutes to get her purse and jacket. She backed her car out of the garage and stopped at the end of the driveway. Mike got in, and she drove him home.

"Thanks, Mrs. Mitchell," he said as he got out of the car.

"You're welcome, son," she replied and drove away.

"Mike! You're limping! What happened?" a concerned Mrs. Hollywell asked.

"I tripped and fell. I twisted my ankle."

"Sit right down here," she ordered. She grabbed two pillows and put them on the sofa. "Put your leg up here. You need to elevate that ankle."

Mike obediently put his foot on the pillows.

"I'll be right back with some ice. Keep your shoe on for now, and we'll ice your ankle for ten minutes. Then I'll take a look at it."

"Mom, it's no big deal," Mike objected.

Mike's mother is a registered nurse and works in a doctor's office. Every injury is a big deal to her. She returned with an ice pack and wrapped it around his ankle with a towel. "How did you get home with an injured ankle?"

"I fell right across from Mrs. Mitchell's house. She came out and insisted on driving me home. You know how she is."

"I'm glad she brought you home. I'll have to thank her."

"I already did, Mom."

"Well, I'll thank her, too. Now, you just sit there with your foot up for a while. Do you want a book?"

"No. I'll turn on the TV. Thanks."

"You're welcome."

Mrs. Hollywell went into her office and made the call, thanking Mrs. Mitchell for driving Mike home. She was not one to forget a kind deed.

After about twenty minutes, a call came from the living room. "Mom, can you hear me?"

"Yes, Mike. What do you want?"

"Can I get up? I need to use the bathroom."

Mrs. Hollywell came into the room. "Stand up slowly. Just put a little weight on it to test it." She pulled a dining room chair over for him to use for support.

"It hurts quite a bit, but I can walk okay. I'll take the chair along with me."

What a sight! Mike walked to the bathroom pushing a high back chair along in front of him. His mother was waiting for him when he returned.

"Sit down and put your foot up." She pulled the chair over by his feet and sat down. "I'm going to take your shoe off. Scream if it hurts."

"Very funny. Please do it slowly."

Carefully, she untied and loosened the laces. Then slowly, she bent the shoe and pulled it off his foot. Mike groaned a little.

"Let me take off the sock," Mike insisted. He pulled his leg up and crossed his injured leg so he could reach his foot. The sock came off easily.

"It's quite red," she commented. "And it's swollen a little. Some of the redness is from the ice. Keep it elevated and we'll ice it for ten minutes. Then we'll remove the ice for twenty minutes. Repeat that for the next couple of hours. Then we'll check it again."

"Can you take us out to Gramma Tessie's house tomorrow? Erika and I were planning to ride our bikes, but I think I better go by car."

"Yes, I can. What time do you need to be there?"

"Erika said we should be there by one o'clock. I'll call and tell her about the change in plans. Can we pick her up on the way?"

"Sure."

Mike called Erika and the plans were changed. Then Mike called J.J. to tell him about the mishap. J.J. said he was sorry to hear about the injury and told him not to worry about a ride home. Someone would take them home, so his mom wouldn't have to make two trips.

After a couple of hours of icing his ankle, Mike got really tired. He ended up napping for another two hours.

"How's that ankle?" Mrs. Hollywell asked when Mike tried to sit up.

"It still hurts a little."

"Here, I got these crutches out of the garage," Mike's dad said. "I found a cane, too. Use whichever one you need."

"Thanks, Dad." Mike got up and decided to use the crutches for now. "It hurts a little more when I put some weight on it."

"Try to stay off it as much as possible. And no swimming tomorrow."

"What?" Mike exclaimed.

"That's right, young man. You stay off that ankle tomorrow and stay out of the water! That's an order from your doctor!" his mother insisted.

"But you're a nurse."

"Close enough! Now, let's have some supper."

Mike was able to get around pretty well with the crutches. He didn't move around much, but the crutches became easier to use with practice.

"I'll be fine tomorrow," he said to his mom as he headed across the room toward the stairs. "Good night."

"Hold on there," interrupted his dad. "You are sleeping in the downstairs guest bedroom."

"Oh, I didn't think about how I was going to get upstairs with these crutches," Mike admitted.

"I'll get your pillow," offered Daryl, Mike's older brother. "Tell me what clothes you want, and I'll get them, too."

"Okay, thanks," Mike replied.

"Good night, Mike," his mother called as he made his way into the guest bedroom.

Daryl returned with the requested clothes and took them into the bedroom. Then he went upstairs to bed.

Mr. and Mrs. Hollywell were sitting in the living room. "Mike's sprain is worse than he thinks," Mrs. Hollywell said.

"How bad is it?"

"If he stays off it and keeps it elevated tomorrow and the next few days, it should heal in a week or so."

"We'll probably have to keep after him about that," replied his dad.

Neither of his parents would understand when they saw Mike Saturday evening. His ankle would be completely healed.

35

DR. M HELPED TESSIE AND GRAMS CARRY THINGS INTO THE kitchen. When they had finished putting the dishes into the dishwasher, the two ladies went to sit down by the lake.

"Sorry to interrupt," Dr. M said as he entered the living room where the reunion was still going strong. "I'd like to talk with the parents for a few minutes. Please follow me. You kids stay here and talk. This will only take a few minutes."

The adults agreed and followed Dr. M downstairs.

. . . .

"Don't say anything." He pulled the lever, and the big wall unit swung out from the wall. Then he put the code into the keypad, and the doorway to the room opened. "Follow me," he said as he entered the room. "Please sit down. This is a control room used to monitor Earth's news and to contact Saros.

"What I am about to tell you may be hard for you ladies to understand. Dale and Harold have been on Saros and understand the situation there. I'll try to keep this as simple as I can.

"As you ladies know, your husbands can trace their lineage back to the planet Saros. The reason we are here is because we are trying to save their dying world. The water supply on Saros will run out in about twenty-five years. Your husbands were instrumental in adding ten of those years. That's why they have been away the past two years.

"Right now, plans are being made by an underground military unit on Saros to invade Earth. They are very powerful and could very well succeed in destroying much of Earth's population. Besides sending some of Earth's water back to Saros, they plan to relocate millions of Saronians to Earth. They have yet to solve the problem of Earth's damaging yellow sun. But I believe they are close. Their invasion timetable calls for a small exploratory invasion to take place in about four months. After they survey the Earth and determine how to proceed, the full invasion force will be sent. They expect that to happen in nine months or so."

"This is rather hard to understand," Janice said. "I can't believe Earth is in danger from a faraway planet."

"What can we do?" Harriet asked.

"You can be supportive of your husbands. I am the one who must try to convince Earth's leaders that this threat is real. Your husbands may be called upon later, but I hope not. I want to protect your families from any ridicule or violence that may result when this becomes public knowledge.

"Most people will not believe it and will dismiss it altogether. Others will call us crackpots and may try to stop us from telling our story. These will be dangerous people. That's why we want to keep you out of it."

"So, what're you going to do?" asked Dale.

"I'm not sure yet. My new magno-pulse machine will now allow me to stay on Earth at least five years. It's safely hidden and well protected. I will destroy it before I let it fall into the hands of those wishing to attack Earth.

"We have a spy working within the PSSG. That's what the underground military is called: the Progressive Save Saros Government. We think he will be included in the first contingent of ships that will arrive here in a few months. If so, he can keep us informed regarding their plans. He may even be able to sabotage the work they do here as well as alter the reports they send back to Saros."

"Do you think we are in any danger?" Harriet asked.

"No," Dr. M quickly replied. "None of you can be recognized as having Saronian blood in you. You will not register on the scanner the three spies brought here from Saros.

"There are three spies staying somewhere around this lake. They used their scanner to locate me. They overheard Tessie talking about a special Saros stone with Henri, and now they are suspicious of both of them. They do not register on their scanners either, so I think everyone is safe.

"I will keep you informed as I learn more. Try not to worry. You will have enough to do adjusting to family life again.

"Major Stromberg has spoken to the owner at the plant where Dale and Harold used to work. They will have jobs waiting for them in three weeks. Hopefully, things will soon get back to normal for all of you.

"Do you have any questions?" Dr. M asked. When no one spoke up, he continued. "Then let's go upstairs. I would like to talk with J.J. and Henri if that's okay. We'll take a walk down by the lake."

Henri and J.J. were sitting on the porch, talking when Dr. M found them. "Care to take a walk down by the lake?" he asked.

"Sure," they replied.

As they walked, Dr. M explained what he had told their parents. Their mothers were not to know about their powers for now. They would need to be very careful when they talk to be sure no one could overhear them.

"We can do that," J.J. assured him. Henri agreed. They all sat down with Grams and Tessie near the water.

"What do you want to do about telling Mike and Erika?" Dr. M asked. "Do you want to talk with them first, or should I discuss their ancestry and then have you talk with them?"

"You talk with them first, Dr. M," Tessie said. "Once they learn about who they are, then J.J. and Henri can talk with them."

"When will you tell them about the Saros stones?" J.J. asked.

"I will explain a lot of things to them. Then I'll let you two talk with them. After that we'll explain about the Saros stones. Then I'll leave. The four of you can talk a while and see how everyone feels," Dr. M continued. "They will be here soon. I'll talk with them about an hour after they get here. Swim and have some fun first. They'll have a lot of questions about the reappearance of your fathers."

"Okay," Henri said, "this should be a very interesting afternoon."

"There's no doubt about that," J.J. added.

They sat there, drinking in the peace and quiet the lake setting provided. They all knew that peace was going to be very difficult to maintain.

Several minutes later, a shout came from near the house. "Hey! Can I join the party?" Mike hollered.

"Me, too!" Erika added.

"Sure," J.J. called out. "Come on down."

Slowly and carefully, Mike used his crutches to navigate the gentle slope down to the lake. Erika walked beside him. They finally got to where the others were sitting.

"Mike!" J.J. exclaimed. "You're on crutches! I didn't know it was that bad."

"What happened?" Henri asked.

As Mike eased himself into a chair, he explained, "I was jogging along the sidewalk near Mrs. Mitchell's house when I saw two walkers. I jogged out into the grass to miss them and another runner cut me off and tripped me. I went tumbling. My ankle was twisted and is still very sore."

"Who would want to trip you? And why?" J.J. asked.

"It was a cocky kid named Hunter. I met him while running around the track. He wanted to race, so we did one lap. He's the fastest runner I've ever seen. I was running as fast as I could, and he raced past me twenty yards from the finish line and laughed the whole time.

"Then he showed up ten minutes later in front of Mrs. Mitchell's house. He must have been watching me. He cut across in front of me, so I tripped. He laughed again and said, 'Now I know you're not a runner.'"

"Well, let's forget about him and enjoy the lake," J.J. suggested.

"Can you swim?" Henri asked.

"No. Dr. Mom has forbidden me to even get near the water. I am probably already too close to it. Don't tell her."

"She should know what's best for your injury," J.J. said. "You had better do as she says."

"Oh, I intend to. But what fun can we have if we don't swim?"

"You'll be surprised at all the excitement we've got in store for you," Henri said. "Here comes Dr. M. I think he'll get us started."

"Right you are, Henri," Dr. M said. "I know you just sat down, Mike, but I'd like you and Erika to walk back up to the house with me. I'd like to show you something and tell you a little story."

After they had gone into the house, J.J. said, "I'd sure like to see their reaction when Dr. M talks about their ancestors. Do you think they will believe him?"

"No," replied Henri. "I'll bet Grams, Tessie, and Dr. M will have to reveal their Saronian forms before they believe anything."

....

A half hour later, Dr. M came out and asked J.J. and Henri to join him. "They're all yours," he said to them. "Good luck!"

"What did they say?" asked J.J.

"They didn't believe anything I said. I didn't tell them much. Start out by telling them your fathers have returned. Don't explain anything about that, except to say that you can tell them later. Say there is something much more important to talk about."

"Okay," J.J. and Henri replied together.

36

DAG AND JOE WERE WALKING BACK TO THEIR MOTEL AND enjoying the weather. It was a beautiful summer evening.

"Did you notice anything unusual about that kid who tripped Mike?" Dag asked.

"Now that you mention it, he seemed to have a glow about him. I did not really think about it because he ran off so quickly."

"Yes. That is what I saw, too. He had a golden glow that seemed to be all over him. I have not seen anything like that here on Earth."

"What do you make of it?" Joe asked.

"I read something many years ago when I was in school on Saros. There were writings that described legendary beings who lived on Saros hundreds of years ago. They had super strength and speed. They made life miserable for everyone around them. They demanded to be treated as kings and made people wait on them. They killed people who did not do what they were told to do. The books said they were evil."

"What happened to them?" Joe wanted to know.

"The stories said most of them lost their powers when they got older. And they disappeared. No one could explain what happened to them."

"Do you believe any of that?"

"Well, they are just legends. However, many legends are based somewhat on facts. I had a teacher who told of a very old prophecy. It predicted one young person who developed his powers between the ages of fourteen and fifteen. The stories said he would cause a lot of trouble, be involved in an interplanetary war, and would be defeated by a mystical group of four kids born on a faraway planet."

"I have heard enough," Joe said. "I think I will stop by McDonald's and eat before going home."

"Okay. I will go with you."

The restaurant wasn't very crowded. They got their food and sat down in a booth to eat.

"Look over there," Dag said as he pointed across the room. "See the glow around that kid in line? He is the one we saw earlier."

"Yes, that is him. That glow is quite bright. I wonder if Earth people can see it. He is the only one I have ever seen who has it."

"Hey! You can't cut in front of the line! See these people? They were here first!" a big man who looked to be in his mid-twenties said to Hunter.

"Mind your own business!" Hunter growled. "I'm in a hurry, and I'll be next." He took a step toward the cash register.

As the clerk said, "Next, please," the man grabbed Hunter by the arm and pulled him back. That was a mistake.

Hunter, who was just a little taller than the man, put his right hand under the man's chin and lifted him off the ground as if he were weightless. An ugly, guttural growl escaped Hunter's lips. Then he spoke.

"I'll put you down. And you shut up! If I hear another complaint from you, I'll throw you across the room! Do you understand?"

"Y-Y-Yes, I do," stuttered the man.

The other people in line just stared. No one said a word. There was something about the kid that seemed threatening and dangerous. They wanted no part of it.

Hunter walked to the register, made his order, and moved aside. His order came up quickly, and out the door he went.

"Did you see the strength that kid had?" Joe asked.

"Yes," Dag replied. "I also saw how fast he ran when he left after tripping Mike. We must find a way to talk with him. If he has special powers, we might get him to help us. He could be a valuable asset if we have a war. I wonder if he has other powers.

"That glow sure is weird. I will send a message to the general and tell him what we have seen. I will ask for some information regarding the legends. I wonder if this kid could somehow be related to Saros."

"I do not see how that could be possible. I would like to get the car and drive by the lake on our way to the cabin," Joe stated. "I would like to see the water again."

"Okay," Dag said.

They parked the car when they got to the lake and walked down to the water. They sat down at a picnic table.

"This sure is a nice lake," Joe said thoughtfully. "I could like living here."

"Well, do not get too comfortable," Dag cautioned. "Remember that the yellow sun is slowly killing you."

"That scares me. What if the ship does not come to get us in two months?"

"Then we become casualties of war. I want to get some good information to send back to Saros first. I want to help get water for our planet."

"Okay. Then what do we do next?"

"We do nothing until Captain Monteford's week is up. Then we will send a message to the base. Colonel Jabu will tell us what to do then. I want to go back to Tessie's house and listen some more. I think we will get some good information from her if we are patient."

They talked some more and then drove back to their cabin. They talked on the way about meeting Mike and Mrs. Mitchell.

"Do you think Mr. Mitchell will have a job for one of us?" Joe asked.

"He might. Tomorrow we will go talk to him."

"Which one of us takes the job if he offers it to us?"

"I do not care. Do you want to work there?"

"Sure," Joe replied.

"Okay. Then the job is yours," Dag said.

Both men were surprised when they saw two cars coming toward them on the single lane dirt road near their cabin. "Quick. Turn right onto the next road ahead." Dag ordered. "I see some more cars coming from the road where our cabin is."

Joe turned just as two police cars came up from behind and went straight across the road they had turned on. Then they heard a siren and saw a fire truck coming.

"I wonder what happened," Joe said.

"Drive away from here but not too fast. We do not want to have to answer any questions."

When they turned left again, they saw the smoke. It was coming from the area near their cabin.

"I hope that is not our cabin burning," Joe said. "How can we find out what happened?"

"We will go back to the motel. We can drive around the area tomorrow. We can eat breakfast in the restaurant in the morning and ask about the police cars and the smoke."

The next morning brought news of the fire. Several men were having coffee and breakfast at the nearby restaurant. Joe and Dag took a booth right next to the tables where the men were sitting.

"Was there much damage?" one of the men asked.

"Two cabins burned to the ground. The fire spread through some trees close to one cabin, and a second one, up the road and around a curve, caught fire before the fire department could get there. Luckily, they carry fire retardant with them and were able to spray several other trees nearby. There was a helicopter just leaving the airport five miles away. It was able to load up with fire retardant and get to the fire within ten minutes. They contained the fire by dousing the area around the two burning cabins. They figured some burning embers blew onto the roof of the second cabin. The entire area could have burned."

"That's the best news of all. Well, that and the fact that no one was injured. I bet the owner of the second cabin is going to be upset when he hears about this."

"I heard the police say they think that cabin has been abandoned for some time. They don't know who owns it."

Another man added, "The fire department does a great job. They got there fast and protected everything nearby, as well as putting the fire out."

"Did you hear how it started?" the first man asked.

"Yes. A lady was frying steaks on a griddle on a big outdoor grill. When she tried to lift the griddle, the handle was so hot she couldn't hold it. Somehow, she knocked the grill over. It landed against the house and caught some stacked newspapers on fire. She couldn't find a hose, so all she could do was call 9-1-1. Luckily, she had her cell phone with her."

That was all Dag and Joe needed to hear. Now, they were really worried. The second cabin that burned could have been theirs.

"What will we do if our cabin is gone?" Joe asked. "We will not be able to contact the base. Our radio was in that cabin."

"There is nothing we can do right now," Dag said. "Keep your voice down. We do not want anyone to hear us. We will drive out there after we eat."

They took their time eating. Since they couldn't cook at the cabin, most of their meals were at fast food places. Sitting inside a restaurant was very nice. Money for their food was not a problem because of the duplicated cash Zolar had made for them.

They paid their bill and slowly drove out to the lake. Hopefully, there would not be a lot of people looking at the burned cabins.

Fortunately, they met no cars as they approached the single-lane turnoff. Once on the road next to their cabin, they pulled off into the deserted little lane by some bushes.

There were large tire impressions in the roadbed. It looked like some big truck had recently driven back here. There were also a couple of empty lots where the grass had been flattened.

"This does not look good," Dag commented.

"I agree," Joe replied.

They parked and walked along the seldom-used trail that now was covered with large tire tracks.

"Oh!" a startled Dag groaned. "Our cabin is gone! It has burned to the ground!"

"What will we do?" Joe asked.

"First, we need to get out of here. We do not want to be asked why we are here. There is nothing left, but I am sure our money is safe where we buried it."

"How will we contact the base?" Joe asked again.

"Dr. M must have a way to contact Saros. Captain Monteford had a radio, too. Now, I hope the soldiers do return. Without them we are doomed!"

The two men walked back to their car and drove to the motel. Neither man said a word. They were in shock.

After sitting in their car for several minutes, they went inside to ponder their desperate situation.

TO BE CONTINUED

THE FOLLOWING IS AN EXCERPT FROM BOOK THREE.

"YOU'RE JUST MAKING ALL OF THIS UP," SAID MIKE.

"Why would we lie to you?" Henri asked. "Mike, my power allows me to turn time back one hour. I am the only one who knows that one hour of time is being relived. That's how I knew the branch would break. It broke when you reached out and grabbed it. You fell to the ground and died. I cried and then remembered the bracelet. I figured I had nothing to lose, so I pressed my thumb onto the stone in my bracelet and hoped for the best. It reset time back one hour. That is why I climbed the tree by that branch. I had to keep you from grabbing it."

"I still don't think any of this is possible," Erika said.

"Did Dr. M tell you about Saros?" J.J. asked. "Did he tell you he's from there? Remember the seemingly magic train in the 'cabin' at school? We even talked about how Dr. M seems to be in the right place to help out at times. We wondered if he had special powers."

"Yes," replied Mike. "We didn't believe that either."

"I think a demonstration is needed," J.J. said. "But first answer this question. If Dr. M is from another planet, and that planet is considering a war with Earth to take our water, would you two be willing to help us? Because of your Saronian ancestry, you two have been chosen to receive Saros stones that will give you special powers, too."

"Now you're talkin'!" Mike exclaimed. "What kind of powers?"

"Mike!" Erika said, raising her voice a little. "You don't believe this, do you?"

"Wouldn't you like to have special powers, Erika?" Mike asked.

"I don't know. What kind of power are you talking about, J.J.?" Erika asked.

"Only Dr. M knows that. He has the Saros stones. You didn't answer the question," Henri reminded them.

"I guess...I would," Mike said slowly. "I just don't believe any of this time-stopping stuff is possible. Although that breaking-branch exhibition was impressive."

"I'd want to help, but what could I do?" Erika wondered.

"I'm going to get Dr. M and have him give you a demonstration that should convince you both. I think Grams and Gramma Tessie will be involved, too," J.J. said, a little perturbed. He didn't like not being believed.

He returned a few minutes later. It was a little crowded with seven people in the secret room.

Dr. M spent nearly twenty minutes going over the entire situation on Saros. He explained how the kids were related to the first people who came to Earth from Saros. Their eyes got a little larger as he explained that both Grams and Gramma Tessie had Saronian blood in their veins.

"This is just too much!" Erika shouted as she burst into tears.

Vocabulary for Book # 2

1. defibrillator: He quickly opened the *defibrillator* case and took out the unit.
2. paramedics: The new voice told her that the *paramedics* had arrived.
3. unscrupulous: He knew there would be *unscrupulous* people who would want to use his power for greed.
4. enigmatic: . . . as an *enigmatic* expression appeared on his face.
5. aghast: J.J. was *aghast.* Grams sounded like she knew a lot more than she was telling.
6. tenuous: His *tenuous* hold over his emotions gave way, and a tear slipped out of his eye and ran down his cheek.
7. scrumptious: "That apple pie was *scrumptious*."
8. incredulous: He was *incredulous.*
9. admonishing: Then J.J. remembered Grams *admonishing* him not to try to look for ways to use his power.
10. premonition: "Is this a *premonition*? Am I sensing the future?"

11. statuesque: She approached the *statuesque* deer.
12. credence: ". . . lends *credence* to the idea that Mike is the one."
13. susceptible: This made them less *susceptible* to the damaging yellow rays of Earth's sun.
14. infiltration: "Continue with the *infiltration* training."
15. unsavory: Deep in the woods in an old abandoned cabin a few miles from Gramma Tessie's house, three *unsavory* characters were gathered.
16. surveillance: "We must set up *surveillance* on his house.
17. circuitous: The next day, Tessie took a *circuitous* route to Grams' farm.
18. ransack: "We'll tie her up and then *ransack* the house."
19. tentatively: "I did," Mrs. Jamison *tentatively* spoke up.
20. translucent: The glow faded and Dr. M was pushed back through the *translucent* wall.
21. aperture: He put his face up to a small *aperture*.
22. anomaly: Dr. M was aboard the spacecraft heading to check the *anomaly*.
23. ruse: "The anomaly you saw was a *ruse* to get you out here."
24. potable: "We know about the mission to Neptune and Uranus to determine if the frozen water is *potable* and could be transported to Saros."
25. thwart: "If we can *thwart* their preliminary plans, we might be able to stop the invasion."
26. camaraderie: "It's good that you know about each other. It will build *camaraderie*."

27. disintegrate: "It will *disintegrate* everything within fifty yards of it. There will be nothing left of the house or the cars."
28. exasperated: "The ammonia and methane are inseparable," an *exasperated* Dale finally said.
29. deftly: A tear started down his cheek, but he *deftly* used a tissue to blow his nose and intercept it.
30. incredulously: Henri finally spoke. "Mike and Erika?" she asked *incredulously.*

Made in the USA
Lexington, KY
27 March 2015